THE COWARD

A novel

KYLE R. BULLOCK

May God bless
you, keep you, and
shine upon you always.

KB 3/14

DEDICATION

This is for you, Poppy.
You will always be a hero to me, no matter what. Thank you.

CONTENTS

ACKNOWLEDGMENTS

First, I must thank Terry Bullock and Cynthia Botello for teaching me about writing, showing me how to write well, and most importantly, encouraging me to share my writing with the world. To Devon – you were always supportive, patient, and loving throughout the entire process and I love you dearly! Thank you for your help throughout this whole thing. My very special thanks also goes to Chris Marks, Elliott Metherd, Liz Huddle, and Nathan Richardson for your incredible contribution to this book. Without you, this would not have been possible.

And finally, my deepest thanks to all the heroes out there who make stories like this possible. Thank you for living with the kind of faith that makes the world a more joyful place to live.

PART I

ONE

His long, sturdy jaw line clasped his lips around a flimsy cigarette as he peered out over the great Pacific. His quivering eyes gazed nervously at the rising sun in the east. The Hawaiian bank was being lapped gently by a smooth tide and the quietness of the waters was chilling. It had not been that way forever and it was one of the last times he was going to see a beach this quiet ever again.

It was the late part of March, 1943. In a few short weeks, Lieutenant John Burke was going to be shipped onwards to Guadalcanal in the Solomon Islands, a haven for Allied soldiers and home to thousands of fighting men in the Pacific front. It was going to be, after all, where they were going to be killing Japs, so it was a sensible place to end up.

Nearly four hundred men from Burke's quadrant were making their way through the last part of flight training, most of which were still wet behind the ears. As they would line up in the morning, Burke often wondered if any of them had ever taken a beating in their life outside of boot camp. None of the men had been more scared in all their lives. In fact, Burke often wondered how the punks even passed boot camp. *He* barely made it and he had the likes of his mother and old man McDuff to prepare him for the Air Force before he shipped. These kids had never so much as thrown a punch on the schoolyard let alone shot a man before ending up on the front lines of combat.

Of course, there were the Navy brats from the *USS Enterprise* who had just come off of a win in the Pacific, off the coast of the Marshall Islands. They intermingled with the Air Force boys only to remind the boys of their victory across the threshold. The Navy thought they were hot stuff, sitting pretty in the Big E. If only they could have known what was waiting for them in the months to come. The Navy brats would sit around in their barracks talking as if they had already won the war. They just pissed Burke right off, but then again, neither Burke nor his squadron had even seen action yet. They could only sit and listen to the jeers and laughter of the cocky Navy men basking in another one of their "game changing" victories.

There were twelve men in Burke's squadron who flew and trained together. The men were close, but Burke especially palled around three of them. First, there was Lucky. His real name, of course, was Larry – or Gary or something with an "r" in it. To the men, he was unquestionably "Lucky." Everybody on base who flew always had someone named Lucky flying next to him; somehow they believed flying next to someone named Lucky might actually bring them luck, although it seemed that it rarely did. Burke's Lucky, though, was actually Lucky. He was originally from California somewhere and seemed to have come having weathered a few more storms than the rest of the squad. The stories went that when he was 7, he survived a train car accident that killed a group of fine, God-fearing people, leaving him with only a gash below his lower lip. When he was 12, he fell out of a moving vehicle and down the side of a cliff. He didn't even break a bone but walked away with a matching gash above his left eye. By the time he had made it into the Air Force with the rest of the men, he was an ugly son of a gun who had seen his fair share of fights and bloodshed. Somehow though, underneath his sandpaper exterior, Lucky was as laid back as a hammock. The rest of the squad figured if Lucky could have survived even half of all that he was rumored to have survived, he would have probably survived falling out of the sky if the time came for it.

The second of the group was an Italian from the northeast – a short, stocky sort of fellow with righteous temper and thick, grizzled voice named Ettore. As an Italian, Ettore did not initially receive a warm welcome into the military. Since Italy had sided with Germany and the other Axis powers, Ettore had faced more prejudice stateside than he cared to stomach. As a result, Ettore channeled his frustration towards patriotism. By the time he had entered the Air Force, Ettore was so patriotic, no man even dared *joke* about his allegiance.

His name, of course, still sounded Italian, which meant that every once and a while, someone would spout off about him being a traitor. This usually ended with that person's face implanted in the ground with Ettore's fist. One day, as a joke, one of the men called Ettore "that Mexican, Hector," and while he hated being mistaken for a Mexican, it was better than being called a traitor, so he allowed it and the name stuck.

Hector had a way of intimidating just about anybody into doing just about anything, and half of the time it was unintentional. He was a tough bastard, no doubt about it. He had a look in his eye that would have shot a bird right out of the sky.

Then there was Leo. He was a young kid, like Burke. According to his tags and records, Leo was the same age as Burke — who was already one of the youngest in the squad. Leo was certainly the *least* daring of the group by a long shot. This was accentuated in his features — deep set eyes, lanky torso, smooth jaw, and large, round ears. Somehow, Leo's body was in constant disrepair and this got him out of countless training runs. During one of the training runs, Leo copped out by telling the doctors he thought his appendix was about to burst. The second time he used the excuse of the appendix, the doctors were less sympathetic. The third time he used the excuse, the doctors told him the best medicine for a hurting appendix was to do training runs. The men were damned when his appendix actually did burst two weeks later. Bastard wasn't lying.

Of course, there was Burke's commanding officer, Major Allison out of Garden Valley, Idaho. He was a tall man with a barrel for a torso and lead weights for heels. His squinted, narrowed focus allowed him to see nearly every detail on and off the battlefield. Major Allison flew crop dusters for several years before the war in Europe got started. His daddy before him was a tough-as-nails veteran and his daddy before him could make a strong man go weak in the knees with nothing but a glance. When Major Allison entered the Air Force, he was the toughest old coot the army had ever seen, born and bred. He never said much, either, and all the men figured they knew why too. By the time he was stationed in Hawaii in 1941, he'd helped deliver arms to the Allies in Europe enough times to know what the feeling of a bullet grazing past your wing felt like. When the Japs flew in on December 7, well, no man who survived that ever lived the same afterwards. The word amongst the men was that Major Allison had shot seven birds out of the sky himself, two with nothing more than small arms fire from his primary. Burke had always doubted that story but wisely kept his mouth shut about it. For Burke, it didn't quite matter if any of the stories were even remotely true; Major Allison still had a way of scaring the hell out of him just by the way the Major ate his breakfast – silent, cold, alone.

Burke flicked out his cigarette into the waves of the ocean and made his way back to the landing strip. It was a short, terrifying little strip of concrete that was but two inches short of being a safe landing zone. Most of the first time pilots, like him, were less concerned about the Japs as they were concerned about making a safe landing. He was scared to wits, as most of them were. Once strapped into their planes, every button, switch, and lever did something that could have potentially dropped each of them out of the sky like a lead paperweight. It was incredible, Burke thought to himself, wearing a crooked, childish smile. The men were about to take off, fly in formation once around the island, and come back down safe and sound. Such would be the briefing, anyways. Burke left the briefing trembling, his hands shaking violently as he attempted to strap his helmet on over his head nearly giving himself a headache doing so. Burke glanced behind him as he stumbled towards his plane and caught a glance at Leo, who was already staring at his controls, his face pale white and jaw hanging wider than the Carlsbad Caverns. The kid was nervous, to say the least. Behind Leo, Hector flung himself excitedly into his cockpit while tossing an insult towards Leo. "Come on, flyboy!" he shouted. "Are you an eagle or a chicken!?"

Leo ignored Hector, oblivious to anything but his fear of heights, a fact that Leo had always wished he would have considered more before enlisting in the Air Force.

"What do you say, John," Hector shouted at Burke, "We're finally doin' it!"

"Yeah, we are," he replied as it all sunk in.

Flying in front of Burke was Lucky. Lucky had managed to put on his helmet , sit down, and lean back all in one move. It was as if he had done this hundreds of times before and it now all came as a major inconvenience to him. The look in Lucky's eyes was fixated, concentrated, calmly at the controls of the plane while his hands caressed the gunner controls righteously. Burke had always figured that somewhere along life's path, Lucky had seen his fair share of death. He had to have. Every man in the squadron who heard it had bought Lucky's story about the train car accident and motorcar story – except Burke. Burke knew that cool-as-steel look in Lucky's eyes was a cover story for something much more sinister in his past.

Burke knew the gashes on Lucky's face weren't in the shape of an accidental tumble, but were in the shape of a broken beer bottle. Burke knew, because he had seen it before. Burke was never quite sure what happened to Lucky before the war; whatever it was, it was no accident.

Major Allison marched down the airfield towards his plane, his stone cold countenance chilling the earth beneath him as he moved. His boots carved a path in the hard ground with every deliberate step he took. He didn't say a word. He just got in his plane, gave the signal, and the squad kicked into motion. Burke flew behind his controls and frantically prepared for take-off. None of the men were going to shoot anything on that first run, but to Major Allison, it didn't matter. Each man was going to be trained to rein lead and fire from those planes. Each time they went up in the air meant that they were going to kill better than the day before. Some of the men in the squad thought that Major Allison's coldness was because of his determination to fight better up in the air. Burke knew better than that. He and Major Allison had only a few things in common. One of the things they shared was their holy, reverent fear for what they were doing. It scared the hell out of both of them, knowing that from behind the plane's controls, they held the keys to life or death for the people on the ground.

That first flight up off the ground was altogether terrifying and amazing. Burke flew. All by himself. As the plane lurched upward and leveled to the hum of an incredible engine, Burke's trembling fingers grew calmer, steadier. The muscles underneath his eyes relaxed and his jaw grew lax as the clouds sailed past him like puffs of smoke. Beneath him was a world he didn't belong to. Somewhere, in a ditch or dank alleyway, the man who hurt him most looked up in a jealous fit. His son was flying, and there was no room in the cockpit to tell him what to do. There was no one to throw an empty beer bottle against his head or tell him of their disappointment in him. Burke was flying, where only the angels used to grace. Deep down, Burke hated having to wear a patch on his chest just so he could fly. He always wished that he could have just flown on his own, no one to tell him where to fly or where to land. He wished that he could have flown his plane and never have to shoot a thing. But as God himself had it, if Burke wanted to fly, he had to shoot. There was no way around it. And for that first training flight, nothing was more precious than the calmness of the skies and the peace of the clouds.

At the apex of their flight, Burke lined up his craft alongside Leo and Lucky's planes. Somewhere out there was Hector's craft, flying confidently and courageously towards the battle. Leo was probably out there, gripping the handle of the controls with white knuckles and a holy fear. Lucky – well Lucky was probably as determined as he ever was. For all of them, flying had turned them into little kids. It was the most incredible feeling any of them had ever felt until God himself put each of them to a peaceful rest. Leading the formation was Major Allison. Burke wondered what he was thinking up there. As much as he figured, Burke believed there was probably a look of terror behind Major Allison's dark and tired eyes. None of them had any idea what they were being led into, but Allison did. The Major was the executioner, leading a group of damned souls en route to their final days.

After an hour in the sky, the men lined their planes up and came back down, one right after another. Landing was better than any ticker tape parade they could have had. When the wheels touched back down to earth, they knew they had successfully done the impossible – they had defied gravity. They flew! Flying was a miracle made by man that defied the oldest law of the earth. And that, according to natural law, was worth getting drunk over.

"How 'bout it, eh John?" Hector spit out after his fifth beer. "We flew, eh? And y-you know you weren't half bad at it. Leo here was garbage…"

"S-shut up, Hector," Leo said, scrambling for a comeback. Unfortunately, the liquor was working against his already poor jousting skills.

"Tell you what. I'll give you another minute to rip me a new one, eh?" Hector cackled.

"We flew!" Burke shouted, raising his glass. "Shouldn't we toast or something?"

"Hell yeah," Hector replied, sloshing what beer was left in his glass out as he raised it for a toast.

"Here-here," added Leo.

"Who's gonna do it?" Hector asked.

They stood in silence, waiting for a man to step up. "I'll do it," came a low rumble from the corner of the table.

"Lucky? Yea, alright, Lucky has the floor, everybody," Hector announced.

Lucky stood up solemnly, the cold, cool look in his eyes still as present as ever after five rounds of beer. He lifted his glass and paused, searching for the words to say. Finally he said, "To the fallen, to those falling now, and to those yet to fall. God rest your souls. May we join you only when we're old and grey. To the fallen."

"To the fallen" the rest replied solemnly. The chime of clinking glasses filled the bar and Lucky sat back down, satisfied in his speech.

"What a downer," Hector whispered to Burke.

"Come on, it was good," he replied. "Would it kill you to be remorseful for a second?"

"Can't a guy just enjoy getting hammered and not have to worry about the dead and them ghosts and what not? Eh?"

"He's just saying what's on his mind," Burke replied.

"Yeah, well here's what's on my mind – booze," Hector said, shoving another beer into Burke's hands. "Drink up, my man, drink up! Ha-ha!"

In all of his life, Burke had only been incredible drunk twice. Once was the 1960 World Series and the other was that night. And as it blurred into a drunken haze, the last thing Burke remembered was the incredible feeling of being up there, in the air, away from it all, on his own.

The squad flew several more training missions in the following days. Every time they took off and landed, it was like they had landed on a whole new, fresh world again. Before long, though, they started adding bullets. Once the bullets and ammunition started getting loaded, things changed. From then on, once they took off and landed, it was still as if they were landing on a whole new world, only one that had been doused with a little more destruction than when they took off. And before long, their numbers began to dwindle, and the feelings of flight began to change.

TWO

John Oscar Burke was a coward. As long years passed after the war, his old, misty eyes eventually reflected a man afraid to admit his own cowardice. Even in his old age, he desperately wished he wasn't. To his friends, his family, those whom he loved, he was "Pops," the war hero. But make no mistake, John Oscar Burke was a coward, through and through, and he knew it. It takes a man of real guts to admit something like that, and after eighty-three years of long, tired, sleepless nights, Burke knew it was true. He saw it every morning when he looked into the mirror and saw his scarred, ragged face staring back. He saw it in his sunken, tired eyes that aimed the guns and that witnessed the fire he helped reign down. He knew he was a coward when he sat in his easy chair, watching his trembling old hands play with his blissful grandchildren. He knew he was a coward; he remembered it every day he lived after the war, and he knew that he never had the guts to convince the rest of his family that he was.

He especially saw his cowardice in the flag that hung on his dining room wall every morning. It hung there, in the dining room –

a big red, faded circle on a white, tattered backdrop, watching him eat his breakfast every single morning. Years before, his children had dug it up and had it framed for Veteran's Day. They thought it would make him even more proud and the tragedy was, it did make him proud. That was what made the flag so damn awful to look at – it made him proud. It reminded him that he was a coward for the U.S. government and a coward to his people. Regardless, as he would look at that Jap hanging in his dining room – with tattered corners, worn edges, writing scrawled all around it – it made him a proud man. It made John Oscar Burke a proud coward.

Never, in all of his 83 years of living, did Burke ever tell his family how or especially why he got the flag. Never, in all his years, did he tell them the whole truth. And perhaps only now did the truth come out so as to settle an old spirit that gravely needed his rest. For Burke, it was never a point of conversation he felt needed hashing out. That flag hung on his wall for years and as his children and grandchildren looked at it, they too felt proud. Burke never figured it mattered that they knew the truth. Deep down it always worried him that they might find out the truth and that the truth would stop making them feel so proud. Sometimes, things are better left unsaid. Other times, things are better said when there is no one left to say them. So for Lieutenant John Oscar Burke, it was better that they never knew while he was alive. It kept him as a hero.

Only once in his life did he consider telling the truth. It was when the flag was first mounted on his wall, displayed with pride in his living room, where anybody who set foot in his house could see it. The first day it went up, he searched his heart for the words to say and nothing but an empty, silent mountain breeze echoed in his mind. He didn't like it. The flag was never meant to be looked at like a souvenir – not that flag. It was something that if any of the other members of the family understood, they might not have been as offended by his reaction.

"Do you like it, Pops?" one of them asked.

"I-I…" he replied.

"We had it made up, especially for you – what do you think?"

He gave no reply.

Perhaps if they knew they would have understood his fear, his tears, his pain. That was the first and only moment Burke ever considered telling the truth about the flag. It was no war flag. It was something much more haunting.

The thought of telling them, of course, disturbed Burke until nearly his dying breath. It was still best they didn't know, at any rate. One day, one of his daughters brought home a "boyfriend" of hers, some educated hippie fag she had been dating off and on behind their backs. The kid was a long-haired doofus who thought he was the greatest thing since the wheel because he had become fluent in *nine* different languages. This hardly impressed Burke, partly due to the fact that two of the languages were variations of English and one of the languages – Elvish – wasn't even a real language. Somewhere, though, the kid had picked up Japanese and had become pretty good at reading it. The kid stood there, in their living room, wasting valuable space on the earth, ogling the flag. He began to read it out loud, *out loud!* Burke shot up out of his chair and gave the boy a look that he had not given another man since the war. *To read a thing like that out loud, in a God-fearing home...* thought Burke. *Inconsiderate little twit.*

It was then that Burke decided to move the flag further back into the house, into the dining room, where only he and his family could see it. At the time he told his family that he thought it went better in there and that he liked to look at it during breakfast. Truth was he never liked looking at the thing. Up until the day he died, only Burke and that hippie knew why he moved it. It was a matter of respect.

The story of the flag started years before, even before D-Day. The Illinois air was frosty, freezing their shirts to their chests.

"I don't get paid enough for this s—" murmured one of the other workers as he flung another load of elephant dung into the pile.

"Shut up, Marcus, I swear you're getting the best of me," said another.

"What? I don't!"

"Just shut up."

"I got a cousin in Indiana workin' construction getting paid five cents an hour more for the same work. This place is a wash."

"Then go work in Indiana."

"We deserve better. What do you say, huh John? Wouldn't you think?"

Burke heaved a shovel full of dung towards the base of the growing pile. A searing pain from the frosty air shot through his back and up his shoulder.

"I said, don't you think we should get paid a little better? You listening, John?" said the worker.

"Man, he isn't gonna listen to you," replied the other, "he's not gonna waste what breath he has left on you."

"Ah, go to hell."

"Get back to work!" screamed the Irishman. The men scrambled to their posts and continued shoveling. "Wha' got you ninnygizzards in a coup, eh? Ya don't think I be payin' ya what ya' earn? Because from where I be standin', I be seein' a lot *dopin' around!*"

The Irishman stumbled towards the workers who became ever attentive to their shoveling. The stench of cheap alcohol came wafting behind him as he closed in. The Irishman came right up to Burke, who had been shoveling loyally in his boss's presence. "What say you?" demanded the Irishman. "You think I be payin' ya too little?"

Burke shifted his gaze around and eventually got a glimpse of the Irishman's beady, bloodshot eyes. "N-no sir, I don't."

Suddenly the Irishman let out a wicked laugh that shook each of them down to their cores; it was the kind of laugh only a drunkard could yield. "Ye don't think so! Ha!" he shouted stumbling away. "Ye pick up my animal's shite for a livin', ye get *paid* shite for a living. Now get back *to work!*" he screamed, flinging a bottle towards the men. The bottle shattered against the wall, nearly hitting one of the workers, as the Irishman let out another blood-curdling cackle. This was the way it had always been, and the way it always was.

The Irishman's name was McDuff, a sick old coot who ran one of the city's private zoos. He was the kind of man who would hire just about anybody to do just about anything for just about nothing. It was a terrible job, but it was a job nonetheless. Burke and his mother needed the money and given the situation, any job that would hire, even if it were for eight cents an hour, was better than no job. Most days McDuff was usually just pretty drunk, which meant the men would endure mild to moderate verbal abuse, the occasional bottle being flung in a heated moment of passion. Other days, McDuff was a liquor fiend and would find a special "something" to "incentivize" the men to action; on these days, it was as if McDuff had a vendetta against the world and hitting the men would somehow make peace. Still, other days, the old man would get so pushy that Burke would hide out in the old man's office and listen to the radio, just to keep from getting a lick sooner than later. It was nice in there and somewhat warmer than being out in the elements all day. Of course, this pissed McDuff off righteously when he would catch Burke listening to the latest broadcast, but Burke didn't much care. It usually bought him about an hour and a half away from McDuff.

One day, while hiding out in McDuff's office, John listened to the broadcast that changed the world. The war in Europe was spreading fast, like a cancer, and wasn't letting up. The news anchor that day came in fuzzy, the snow barreling down in drifts outside and blowing the radio signals all about. Burke leaned in closer to hear the announcer. Men and women were dying. Children now orphaned. War was heated. John sat entranced.

Suddenly, out from behind, McDuff wailed a beer bottle straight across the back of Burke's head. Shards of dark brown glass fell across the floor and the whizz of McDuff's shoe cut through the air and landed on Burke's gut hard. The old man was pissed, as usual, but this time Burke didn't care. He could still hear the radio broadcast come through. "War in Europe... another wave of violence breaking... orphaned children given to... efforts heating up..." Another kick from McDuff.

"Ye s-sorry, no good, piece of s—" he screamed.

I'm going, John thought to himself. He wanted out, and the military would get him out. What was happening in Europe sounded bad, but Burke selfishly led himself to believe that it was somehow better than what he was experiencing. He quickly gathered up resolve and made his choice: *I'm going, now. That's my out – I'm going!*

John suddenly pushed himself up off the ground and brought McDuff to the floor with what energy he had left in him. "I quit, you sorry sack of crap!" John shouted, taking his fist and planting it across McDuff's face. And that was it. He was off to join the Army. He was going to fly, going to get as far away from it all as he could.

It wasn't even five o'clock by the time Burke had applied, enlisted, and was set to ship. There was no going back, and he wasn't interested in going back. At the time, the only family he had was his mother, who was an even bigger drunk than McDuff was. Burke's father left him and his mother for another woman when Burke was only nine years old. In fact, the last Burke ever heard of his father, or cared to hear, was that his father had ended up in a dank prison cell somewhere in Ohio, most likely in a pool of whiskey. When John eventually told his mother that he was leaving - enlisted in the U.S. military - she flung a plate at his head and screamed, "John Oscar Burke, you're going to end with your ass up in some muddy ditch somewhere, you damn fool." That was all she said, and that was more than John cared to hear. The next morning, his things were packed and he left.

Burke arrived at the airport with nothing but a canvas bag. In it: a change of clothes, a toothbrush, and a Bible, which he kept at the time for reasons he wasn't quite sure of. Some poor old gentleman was handing them out to all of the new enlistments and instead of passing him by, John took it, mostly out of pity. It certainly wasn't out of religious obligation. God had never much been in his life and, he figured, wasn't going to make much of an appearance after he shipped to boot camp. He figured that in case God made a stunning appearance on behalf of the USO, he should at least have been prepared with his bestseller in hand.

Boot camp, of course, was hell. Burke didn't find many friends and friends didn't find him either. Everybody, of course, was just concerned about making it through boot camp alive so that they might have a chance to die doing something actually productive for their country. They would wake up at four in the morning, run until their legs gave out, crawled the rest of the way, and went to bed at one that morning just to wake up the next day and do it all over again. Encouragement such as "Hurry up, you maggot," and "Faster, you sombitch!" quickly became slogans of the boot camp officers.

Eight weeks of hell and torture passed, designed to make death on the battlefield look like a passing fancy. And truth be told, it did.

Eight weeks passed when Burke received word that he had made it – he was going to fly for the U.S. Air Force. And that was it. The pain, the death, the selfishness of those he had left back in Illinois were going to be under him. In his plane, he could fly above it all. At least that was what he thought.

He could not have been more wrong.

THREE

The men trained for little more than a year: test runs, dry runs, and live runs alike. It exhausted them to no end. Some were beginning to think that they would never actually see the Japs by the time they were finally sent over. Weeks before, pilots had taken B17's loaded with a firestorm over Tokyo. The men figured that by the time they actually saw Tokyo with their own eyes, there wouldn't be anything left to bomb. They eventually found out that they weren't all that wrong either.

Occasionally, as men would leave for missions, things would go sour. Twelve men would go up and eleven would come back; this was the worst scenario for the men on the ground to see. It was always better that ten come back, or even nine, rather than eleven. Ten men coming back meant they got pinned and nine or less meant that the enemy had a strategy they weren't prepared for – nothing could be done in either case. When eleven came back, that just meant that one guy ran out of luck. There was no other real way for them to make sense of it. Every man that put their bird up had what it took to bring it back down, no doubt about it. But when eleven came back from an air raid, it was a stark reminder for them all that war wasn't about who was smarter, faster, more agile, or even stronger. It was about luck, plain and simple. War was really about out-surviving your luck, not out-surviving the enemy.

The local bar was filled to the brim every night by officers of every class and rank. There wasn't much more to do on the islands at the time unless any of the men had the patience to woo a native, island girl into a nightcap. Burke did this only two or three times the entire time he was there and even after he did it, he was reminded how much he undervalued Illinois women. The women back in Illinois were at least forgiving enough to leave you your dignity every once and a while. Island women were far less forgiving. This was usually why the local bar was filled to the brim with service *men*. Even so, the bar was always pretty lively. Every now and then, a Navy fishhead would spout off to a pilot something they would regret. Usually, though, things were relatively civil – as civil as they could be, at least.

On nights, however, when eleven men came back, the bar always had a moment where the noise would die down, just for a moment. It was July 1943 the first time eleven came back while Burke was on the island. There was an eerie calm over the bar; an Air Force bubba stood up and raised his glass.

"To Hennesy, who bought the farm and is living with the best of 'em," he said. The room gave a resounding "cheers," raised their glass, and took a swig of their unsterile grog in recognition of their fallen brother.

And that was it. The room picked back up, the men started sagging and swaying as they told dirty jokes. In the corner, a fishhead was pissing off another fairy with one of his tall tales of feigned heroics. At the bar, the bartender pretended not to notice the improprieties and the slow destruction of his bar. It all went back to normal.

That night, after the toast, Leo leaned over to John and began nervously chatting in his ear. "I got a feelin' that our grease monkeys aren't givin' the once over to us all's birds."

"Shut up Leo," Hector shot back. He pushed Leo away from Burke's ear and shoved the kid's beer back into his hand. "Drink up and shut up, will ya?"

"You might should take me more seriously," Leo said. "It's your ass they be puttin' up in the sky."

"And if my ass gets shot down, the last thing I'm gonna be worrying about is whether or not they washed my windows that morning," Hector laughed, condescendingly.

Leo grew more nervous and pushed up against Burke, chattering frantically in his ear trying to get him to listen to his story. "John, I've been catchin' them all grease monkeys screwin' around just about nearly ev'ry time I go by. Now if that don't make you break out in a holy sweat I don't know what would. I mean think about it! They be the ones puttin' us up there, them the last people you want screwin' around."

Burke nodded his head and smiled. Hector grabbed the beer in Leo's hands and used it to push him back in the chair. "Would you shut up?" he barked.

"I'm just saying," Leo told him. "Lucky, haven't you been seen' them grease monkeys screwin' around a whole bunch more than us'al?"

Lucky leaned back in his chair casually, preserving his stern glare towards the middle distance. "Sure, Leo."

"See, Hector, Lucky's seen't it too."

Hector snarled, his knuckles cracking against the glass bottle in disgust. "Shut up, Leo. For the love of mercy from Mother Mary's good graces, shut up. Don't be a dumbass coward over the dumbass grease monkeys, okay? "

Lucky laughed and sucked some more on his beer. "Don't mind him, Leo. Hector jammed a piece of coal up his ass last week - he's trying to turn it into a diamond for that pretty wife of his back home."

"You're a real bastard, you know that?" Hector told him.

"I got some coal in my tent," laughed Burke. "Think we could start a racket with this skill of yours, Hector?"

Hector picked up a bowl of nuts on the table and threw the empty shells and debris at Lucky and Burke. "I'm going to play pool with a Navy brat. At least getting in a fight with *them* would make me feel like I'm doing an actual public service."

Hector stormed over to the billiard tables and yanked a pool cue out of some poor drunk's sweaty palms. Before the night was over, he had broken a cue stick or two over the heads of some Navy brats. According to Hector, some fishheads mistook him for a "Mexicano cúlo" which led to their immediate head adjustment. All of the guys who flew with Hector knew better, that all Hector really wanted to do was to get in a fight and smack a guy around a bit. He needed to do that about once a week or so; somehow, it was therapeutic for him.

Leo was still at the table rambling on to anyone who would listen about how the mechanics were out to get them and eventually wore himself out of conversation and went to the bar to douse his neuroticism with liquor. Lucky and Burke just sat there, staring at the empty, vinyl-sided wall in front of them. It was a big empty wall with one picture – a framed picture of a Hawaiian Hula girl no bigger than the size of a postcard, hanging all alone on the big, blank, lonely wall. Eventually, after staring at the wall for a considerable time, Burke could take it no longer. He turned to Lucky, who was leaning back in his chair and admiring the sole artwork on the wall. With not a care in the world, Lucky sat there, with a grin on his face that would win a hundred virgin's hearts to him in a moment's notice.

"Why are you not more scared of becoming mission ready than the rest of us?" Burke asked him.

Lucky just sat there, staring at the photo. Finally, he did a double take and looked back at Burke. "Excuse me?" he asked.

"I asked you why you aren't more scared of being mission ready?"

"I don't know, John. Maybe it's because it gets me off the

ground and away from the bar more. I don't know."

"I'm serious," Burke prodded. "I mean, it's okay to be nervous. I'm sure I speak for the rest in saying that we are. What's going through your mind that you're not scared?"

Lucky leaned forward and set all four legs of his chair firmly on the ground. "I just have a sweet disposition, what can I say, flyboy?"

Burke sat back and nodded. Deep down, he knew better and Lucky also knew that he knew better. "Come on, seriously?" Burke eventually replied. "Why aren't you scared? We could start flying the real deal any day now, doesn't that make you turn over at night a little?"

Lucky met Burke's eyes with a fierce gaze. His eyes squinted into darts, bringing the scars on his face closer together, while the bags under his eyes began to twitch. Someplace beneath Lucky's gaze laid a fear, dark and thick. After a moment, he finally replied, "How old are you, kid?"

"How old am I?" Burke replied.

"What, your twenties?"

"Yeah."

Lucky nodded and bit his lip, inspecting Burke with his blazing eyes. As he sat back, Lucky sucked down the remainder of his beer and aimed his head straight at the floor. "Kid," he said. "Sometimes there are things on the ground a whole hell of a lot worse than what's waiting for us up in the air. Live long enough and you'll figure out that getting shot down out of the sky is a merciful way to die." Lucky tossed his beer and lifted the front legs of his chair off the ground, staring back at the picture the rest of the night.

Burke never brought it up again. After all of his 83 years of living, that was the only time Burke ever talked about being scared of flying. He felt it a number of times, but never mentioned it again to anyone. As he sat in his dining room all those years later, staring at the Jap flag hanging drearily in its frame, he realized exactly what Lucky meant. Getting shot down out of the sky would have been a much more merciful way to go.

FOUR

Burke was behind the counter, taking the back off of another television set. It was a long day and the last thing he wanted to do was to have another customer watch him critically as he did what he did best. It had a way of hacking him off more than usual.

"It hasn't been working for some time," the woman said.

"That's okay," Burke said, straining to get the television apart. His neck shot a slight pain down his back that made him shoot right back up. He sighed and rolled his tired eyes.

"I know I should have brought it in sooner, but I just didn't get to it," she continued.

"It really is okay, it won't affect the TV," he replied.

"My husband has been on my back for ages to get it in to have it fixed. I just hope you can fix it."

"I'll see what I can do," he strained, unhooking one of the tubes from the back.

"John? Telephone!" shouted one of the boys in the back room.

"Not now!" he shouted back. "I'm with a customer."

"It's your wife," the kid yelled.

"Tell her I'm with a damn customer!" The woman reeled back in disgust. "I'm sorry," Burke conceded. "Nasty habit."

"She said she really needs to talk to you!"

"Son, I'm busy, tell her I—"

"She said she's going to the hospital, something about a water leak? Hell if I know," said the kid.

"Water leak?" John said. "Water leak. Break. Water break! God, you sonofabitch, kid! She's in labor!" Suddenly, all of the air in his lungs shot out and the world closed in quickly. It was a strange sensation – total terror and total excitement all felt at the exact same time.

"That makes sense," said the kid.

John shot out frantically from behind the counter, not entirely sure where to go next. "I-I'll get to your TV later," he said to the woman. "The kid will write you up. Get up kid, come on! Write her up, write her up!" he shouted as he rushed out the door. Seven hours later, on May 6, 1956, John Burke's first child was born. When he first held his newborn son, life cradled in the palms of his hands, terror collided with pure joy. It was a sensation John felt only a handful of times in his life, and it was the same feeling he had when he was told that he was going to drop bombs on the Japanese for the first time.

For John, flying was like holding his baby in his hands for the first time, watching as it strained to open its little eyes and take in the fearfully big world around it. It was wonderful. But when they loaded the first bomb in his bird's compartment, it felt just like the terror of knowing the power of his actions over that newborn's life to Burke. Life and death were held in the balance of his hands. Burke liked flying before they loaded the bombs. When they started making him take the bombs with him, though, it became a flying torture trap and the most unnerving thing he had ever done in his entire life.

None of the men expected to get the news that they were mission ready so early, especially Major Allison. Every soldier could hear him shouting into the radio set in his office louder than a steamboat the day the call came through. The operator on the other end of the radio told him that orders were sent that flyboys were needed to start a new technique of firebombing later that year. They needed every man that could fly to be up in the air and ready to go when the time came. It was late in the August of 1943. Major Allison, in no uncertain language, told the operator that the men were nowhere close to being ready. Nobody in the outfit took it personally, either. They all figured Major Allison's hope was that they would never have to see the Pacific coastline of their enemy's shores. Major Allison, of course, knew it was mighty high thinking to expect them not to go, but a man such as Major Allison was also a man of faith and hope, even if his faith was a bit outlandish to believe. The operator, in response, told him that there was no reason or use to argue and that it was just better to let it happen. The operator was right, Burke thought. All of the men were confident enough in their flying abilities by then to at least make a trip and land in one piece if left to their own devices. They all knew that they were going to have to pass by the flames of hell sooner or later. It was just a matter of when.

Major Allison came out of his office and carved a path right past the men. He said no words and made no gestures. He didn't even look at one of them. The major just walked on and somehow, all of the men knew what that meant. Various men left to go write their families letters; others went to pray and give their graces to God. A choice few made a beeline for the bar and didn't bother coming out until it was their time to be briefed. They all knew that soon, very soon, the regular bombing runs would be a thing of the past, shoved aside to make room for something much nastier. What it was, no one really knew. Some of the men speculated but nobody asked questions.

Word came round to the men that afternoon that briefing was first thing in the morning. The evening before, as the men made their assorted peace to various parties, Burke headed straight to the barracks. He didn't, of course, have much in the way of faith or family, but he figured he needed to do something. He figured he shouldn't waste three cents to send a letter to his mother; she wouldn't have read it anyways and if something would have happened to him, the United States government would have sent a letter on his behalf for free. Burke's Bible was about the only other thing he had left to look at as a source of hope. He grabbed it and started reading, for the first time:

In the beginning God created the heavens and the earth. The earth was without form, and void; and darkness was on the face of the deep. And the Spirit of God was hovering over the waters.

Burke stopped. For some reason it resonated with him. A lot of men during that time just recited Hail Mary's that the chaplain had taught them to say before their runs. Others would recite prayers they had learned growing up. One of the men was notorious for singing hymns on his way to make a run. Burke figured they did this to absolve them of any guilt and sin they had forgotten to deal with before the run. He didn't do any of it. It scared the hell out of him to think that *darkness* was *over the very face of the waters* where they were flying. Above that darkness hovered a great, big, all-knowing God who just hovered there, as if he were surveillance over what happens above the deep. Sandwiched in between that darkness and God, flying weightlessly in the air, were the Airborne, delivering life or death in their bird's compartment. If something happened up there, they were either going to face the darkness of the surface of the depths or face the God hovering above the waters. Burke always had a fear for them both and decided there in his barrack that he was just going to keep his mouth shut and head down. He didn't want to say anything that would piss off the darkness or God.

Burke sat there, reading his Bible for over an hour the night before the first mission briefing. The next morning, on his way out, he stuffed the small, leather-bound book into the pocket of his jumpsuit uniform. All of the men that morning – including Leo,

Hector, and Lucky – were all a bit morose. None of them had done anything like this before. They had almost all done at least one milk run before, but nothing as big as the mission before them. The air that morning was stale and cold. Salty ocean air crept up their noses and curled their nostrils.

Major Allison finally appeared. His opening comments began with a stern, surveying glare at all the men. It said enough about the situation that they had all got the message. It was a real run, with real ammunitions and bombs. Milk runs and training exercises were a thing of the past. This run was serious. Their target was Tokushima, some 150 miles east of Hiroshima. There wasn't much to the run – fly in formation, drop their cargo, flip, come back home. It was easy to follow. At the end of the briefing, Major Allison looked at the men and with the cold of his eyes watching their souls ever so carefully, he said, "Know thyself. Know thy enemy. And for your eternal soul, know thy God. That is all men."

In Burke's pattern was to be Burke, Leo, Lucky, Hector, and a kid named Parker. He was from Buffalo, a smart kid, one who didn't screw around or fart off. He was straight as an arrow and held his own behind the controls, which squelched the fears of the other men flying along with him. As they were getting ready to climb into their planes, Leo grabbed Burke's arms and pulled him aside.

"John, I dunno, this'is got me. I've been dreamin', ya see, this be nothin' but evil on me all week long," he said.

"What are you talking about Leo?" John replied. "It's going to be fine."

"I've been havin' dreams, John, about fallin' outta this sky. What if this be the day we fall down outta that sky and don't come up? I don't wanna do it, John, I don't wanna fall outta that sky so I don't wanna go up."

Burke looked at Leo compassionately. He felt sorry for Leo, deeply. "Do you have a choice?" he told him. Leo looked back at John with pain and fear, eventually pulling away and walking to his plane like a man heading to his execution.

Eventually, Burke climbed up inside the cockpit of his own plane and strapped on his helmet. In the back of his bird was a hefty, highly explosive amatol bomb. Burke felt the eyes of the bomb staring at the back of his head, glaring angrily at him, and the bomb didn't take its eyes off of him the whole time. Once all the men were loaded, a few said their prayers, Burke kissed the Bible in his jumpsuit pocket, and they all made peace with their Maker.

The flight took what seemed an eternity. The low hum of the engine rattled their heads during the whole flight. The men's formation, though, stayed the course, tried and true. Below them was the black, eternally deep ocean. The surface of the waters were dead still, some small ripples making outcrops here and there. The water looked so deep that if one of them were to drop a quarter in it in 1943, it wouldn't have hit the bottom until 1962. Burke leaned over the controls to peer down into the abyss. He immediately thought of all the men who were floating around down there already. He wondered if they would ever reach the bottom. Burke had never loved water, and this was especially true on this day. There was truly a dark void about the surface of the water, especially as he gazed upon it from way up in the air. He cherished the idea of seeing land again. Eventually land did crop up in the distance, but as it did, the idea of seeing land again wasn't as hopeful as it was over the water. The island before them was a smoldering, grey heap of ash. The sky above the island was charcoal and bitter. The shores were crusty and unwelcoming. Japan looked as though it had become an ashtray that someone kept putting their cigarettes out in.

Tokushima wasn't far from the shore, not but thirty or forty miles inland from one of the island's southern prefectures, which meant the men wouldn't be flying long before dropping their cargo. As they hit the coast of the island, they steadied in formation and barreled down towards Tokushima. Smokey concaves and smoldering piles of rubbles greeted them on the ground all along the path to Tokushima. Burke first saw the city creep up over the horizon right above his control panel. A few intact buildings remained and grew larger and larger as they zeroed in. Burke lined up the city's buildings in his cockpit's reticule. The roar of the engines was deafening. Then, the radio echoed in. "Bomb's away." The lead plane let go, followed by the others. Burke released his cargo – everything in the cockpit went silent. Suddenly, the city of Tokushima disappeared from the reticule of Burke's cockpit and dashed away from sight underneath his control panel. The formation began their flip around a safe distance away from the target. There was a flash, hot red then orange. It darted across the ground beneath their planes before retracting back to the city.

As their planes completed the flip around, there in front of them laid the work of their hands. Brilliant heaps of charcoal rubble, piling up with accents of flaming red and orange flames, sat smoldering beneath the blackness of the ocean in the distance. As the men flew over the city, it disappeared once again from their line of sight, but did not disappear from a single one of their minds. Heaps of smoldering rubble, bodies dismembered and strewn across the streets, and windows bursting with flames – this was the picture of the city the pilots carried with them always. All that remained to be seen on the flight back was the blackness of the ocean void and the ominous glow of heavenly clouds above.

When they had returned, each bird landed as safe and smooth as a song. Everyone got out of their cockpits and set foot on solid ground again. Nobody said a word. Burke climbed out of his cockpit slowly; it felt as though there were lead weights tied to his shoulders that meant to drag him to the ground. Hector marched past him with a fierce burning in his eyes and a haunting smile; he disappeared right away into the barracks. None of the men saw him at the bar for over a week after that; it was as if he no longer needed it. The kid Parker also climbed drearily out of his cockpit and passed by Burke, offering a weak smile and walking on towards the chapel. Lucky and Leo joined with Burke and headed straight for the bar. The three of them passed by Major Allison, who didn't say a word to any of them; the major simply gave them all a nod of affirmation and darted back inside his office.

Once at the bar, Leo, Lucky, and Burke swigged on their beers in total silence. They had been there a whole hour without ordering another beer or saying more than two words to each other. Eventually, another flyboy came hobbling up to their table, stinking of whiskey and urine. He was one of the men they had seen regularly in the mess hall and around the bar. He was a young guy who had been going on mission runs since Burke had arrived on the island. The man yanked a chair away from a nearby table and brought it up to the three others.

"You boys need beer," he slurred out. "More beer. Hey! More beer for my friends here!" The three shied away from him at first, but the man had ordered them a round which meant they all owed him their attention. "Now listen," he began. He leaned in closer, attempting a drunk whisper, "I need… I need some flyboys to help me kick the crap out of a N-Navy BASTARD who keeps stealing my SEXY ISLAND GIRL. Dumb, fishhead… Needs to be taught a lesson about what the Air Force is all about! Courage, right!? Am I right?"

"Look, buddy," Lucky told him. "I think you might have the wrong guys here, check the other side of the bar."

"Like hell I do!" the man shot back. "Meet me out back in twenty and we'll teach the cat a-a lesson." He started to stumble away and suddenly made a double take back to the three. "Oh, b-by the way. By the way – good flyin' today, gentlemen," he said as he tipped his hat to them and returned to the bar.

Leo sat across from Lucky and Burke with a look of concern.

"We aren't rea'ly gonna go fight them boys for 'im, right?"

Lucky and Burke smiled. They all turned and looked towards the man at the bar, where he had immediately passed out. "I don't think so," Burke replied. "I don't think *he's* showing up at the fight, either."

The three sat there, looking at their new beers for a minute quietly. Suddenly, Lucky began to chuckle. "What?" Burke asked.

"At least we got free beer out of the deal," Lucky replied. They all began to smile, even Leo who was slowly relaxing in his chair. And that was that. They drank their beers, walked back to the barracks in peace, and prepared for a new day. From then on, that was how most runs went: they would fly, have their beers, force a few laughs, and go home. Life kept going on.

Years later, Burke sat in his dining room early in the morning, eating stale cereal soaking in a bowl of two percent. The flag, of course, just stared back. Burke slurped another spoonful of soggy corn flakes through his toothless mouth and glared back up at it, thinking of all the runs that went that way, charring the edges of another flag somewhere out in the Japanese forest. He never forgot a single run, although there were many of them. He especially remembered the Shimizu run. None of them forgot the Shimizu run.

FIVE

It was September of 1943. By this time, the men had all been moved to the American base located at Guadalcanal on the Solomon Islands, not far from the coast of Australia and New Zealand. It was a lush island that didn't look much different than all of the other islands. After a while, the men began wishing to end up in the desert, or at least somewhere far away from more green rainforest.

Life in Guadalcanal was no different than it was back on Hawaii or any of the other islands; the only difference was that they were closer to the enemy. That meant they saw a lot more of the enemy and the enemy saw a lot more of them. The military's goal was to edge their way up the Pacific Islands until they finally hit the shores of Japan. New Zealand proved a helpful ally, but only in keeping their heads out of the way. The men also saw a lot more Jarheads on the Solomons than ever before. Before long, more and more Marines began to flood in by the truckload. None of the Air Force became fast friends with the Marines, but they both hated the Navy boys equally, and so decided to be at peace with one another, so long as they had the same "enemy."

Burke was finishing his morning shift, making the rounds and standing post. It was incredibly early, around 0500 hours. Out in the distance, a monkey howled and chattered noisily to the wind while birds cawed wildly back. While it wasn't the heat of August, the cool humidity did not bring much relief; it was uncomfortable and distracting to say the least.

"Sorry I'm late," said Burke's replacement, jogging to his post.

"Yeah," Burke huffed condescendingly.

"Any excitement?"

"About as much excitement as a Wisconsin whorehouse," Burke murmured. His replacement looked back at him puzzled. "No, it was not exciting," Burke explained.

"Oh, gotcha! Be safe, get some rest."

"Yeah, alright," John replied, sauntering back to camp. He was off to enjoy his stony cot back at the barracks and perhaps even have a dream that didn't involve fire or falling or loud noises. Suddenly, he heard a rumble coming in low behind him, drawing nearer. Someone shouted in the distance. Somebody else yelled back. Hair on the back of John's neck stood on end and danced wildly; he didn't even bother to look back. Burke shot down into the trees beside the path and crept down low, cowering there off to the side of the road, covering his head with trembling arms.

The enemy planes soared overhead, followed by a whistle of bombs. Behind him, an explosion shattered the earth and shook the trees overhead. Debris and dirt showered all around him. Fire from the bomb's explosions shot out in every direction from the tops of trees. Before long, the enemy bombers had begun their storm in front of him, delivering their payload quickly before disappearing from sight. Two explosions lit up the sky, one suddenly and the other coming nearly twenty seconds later. Out of the sky fell two of the enemy's giant metal birds. Their remains piled up into burning heaps of twisted, charred metal on the unforgiving ground below. The roaring and crashing continued for a full minute longer; then, as fast as it came in, the noise left.

Behind John, his post was nothing but a heap of chaos. Burke rushed back to where he had been on duty, trying to differentiate the casualties from the rubble. His replacement was on the ground screaming for help, his leg jarred and crushed by the falling debris. Burke rushed over and helped him sit up, moving rubble and dragging him back onto the road. The man's face was bloodied by shrapnel and tree bark. Tears began to stream down his cheeks, dragging the blood down his long, dirty face. The soldier's leg was a mess. Burke thought it looked as though someone had squeezed the bones out of it and left it still attached to his body. Down the road, a medical jeep tore up the dirt path, carving out divots and trenches with its tires, on its way to aid the men. Burke stood up and shouted, waving it down for the man lying at his feet in pain and fear. The jeep pulled up alongside them and a medic darted out of the vehicle even before it had made a complete stop. Two more men jumped out of the jeep with a board and began loading the man onto it carefully.

Burke backed away slowly, watching them take the poor man's twisted body and place it delicately on the board.

Suddenly, the medic grabbed John from behind. "You okay, soldier?" he asked. Burke nodded, still dazed from the confusion of the attack. "You need to go back with us, you need to get patched up," the medic shouted. It was hard for Burke to hear him; the ringing in his ears had not yet dissolved.

Burke shook his head and tried to ask why. "Your face!" yelled the medic. Burked reached up and touched his cheek, which seared in pain. All of a sudden, Burke felt his whole face burning. Somewhere in the chaos a piece of wood had cut his face badly. Blood dripped down his chin and stained the toe of his shoe. Burke looked behind him at all the damage his old post took; it was gone, totally gone. Without thinking twice, Burke piled into the jeep and rode along with the rest of them to the medical tent back at camp.

It wasn't long before they patched up his face. Burke's post replacement managed to make it through several procedures and keep his leg in the process. Burke watched as they patched up his leg, breaking and shoving it back into place. It was a sight he never forgot. Outside, the damage was minimal, but the men were still picking up pieces of broken or dismantled objects. For the most part, the enemy had managed to miss their target by a long shot. Perhaps they had been rookies too afraid to get any closer to the base. Things here and there had sustained some damage, but only from the outskirts of the blast. Burke spotted Leo and Hector running around outside the barracks. Hector was in an excited frenzy, eyeballing the sky and hopeful for more. Leo ducked down beside him. "John!" Leo cried when he spotted Burke outside the medical tent. "You al'right?"

"Yeah, I'm fine," he replied.

Hector marched over to Burke and came to a wobbly stop. He was dancing back and forth anxiously on both feet. "Damn Japs didn't even give me a chance to shoot at 'em, couldn't even make it over to me so I could go to work on them!" he said, spitting furiously.

"Is everybody inside okay?" Burke asked.

"Yeah," Hector said. "They missed us. Just pissed us off is what they did. Makes you want to slap a Jap, eh?"

"Yeah sure," Burke replied. Deep down, Burke knew he didn't. The only thing he felt like doing that morning was to make his peace with God. *I don't know if the Creator deals in luck*, he thought, *but I don't want to use all mine up on the ground.* Burke grew more and more nervous as he watched Hector dance around and eyeball the sky excitedly, and Leo's fearful antics were not helping.

"I need to go," Burke said, his words falling on deaf ears. The other two continued to search the skies and dart around the camp, surveying the aftermath. Burke set out towards the chapel, his knees shaking nervously. On his way to the chapel, he passed by Lucky who was just sitting on the ground, leaning against the exterior wall of the barrack, smoking a cigarette. His eyes were cool but his hand was trembling. Neither man said a word.

The chapel was surprisingly full – possibly five or six men sitting in the room rather than the one or two who usually frequented it. Of those one or two, the kid Parker sat faithfully in prayer in what was probably his usual spot. He had his head bent down in prayer like the good Christian soldier he was, unaware of the others around him. Up at the front, the chaplain was praying a prayer of peace. *Peace will do me no good if there isn't a prayer for luck*, Burke thought.

He took a seat next to Parker, who looked up reverently and gave a friendly smile before returning to his prayer. Burke sat awkwardly in the chapel, feeling more alone than he had in a long time. It wasn't the first time he had been in a chapel. Once, when his grandmother had passed away while he was still young, his mother actually left him at the church after the funeral while she returned home and doused herself in wine. This time, though, was different. It was as if he was actually supposed to *talk* to God, not just merely be in his "house." Burke leaned over to Parker and whispered, "You're here a lot, right?"

"Excuse me?" Parker replied.

"I said, you're in here, in the chapel a lot, right?"

"I guess you could say that."

"You believe in God? You're religious I take it?"

Parker smiled at him. "Yes, you could say that."

"I see," Burke told him. "I just had to ask. I know some of the guys like to come here to get wasted on the free communion wine after hours, so..." Parker just nodded back at him with a friendly smile. "Listen," Burke asked him. "I don't do this whole religious thing a lot, at least I haven't. What do I say?"

"To God?" Parker replied.

"Yeah to God. What do I say to him?"

"Just tell him what's in your heart."

"He won't get mad if I tell him something he doesn't want to hear?"

Parker shook his head in sincerity. "God is never mad at hearing your voice. He is slow to anger and slow to wrath."

Burke nodded cautiously. "You think he'd cut me a little more luck if I asked him for it?"

Parker smiled again. "I think he would extend you more grace if you asked for it, yes."

Grace – religious folk's word for luck, Burke figured. "Do I just start talking to him?" he asked Parker. Parker nodded and returned to his prayers. Burke nodded as well, slowly bowing his head, bobbing his eyes up and down to scan the room and make sure he was doing it correctly. *God,* he said to himself. *I don't know if you do luck. If you do, I need it. If I have to do something to get it, I don't know – let me know. But if you'd rather do this grace thing, do that. Whatever you do, just do it, for me. Got it?*

Burke sat up. The chapel was a calm place, the only calm place at the camp. It was a nice place, he figured. He felt quite opposite towards the medical tent. The medical tent was the last place Burke ever wanted to go to get patched up again. The medics always had bodies piled in the back as if to remind the rest of the men still alive that any one of them could and probably would end up there one day. The chapel at least didn't have dead bodies lying in it, just dead souls frantically asking to be woken up.

Three days after they sustained the attack on Guadalcanal, the men were back up, flying another mission. It was the Shimizu run, as it was later remembered. It was the same as usual – accompany a bomber out to the city of Shimizu right in the center coastline of Japan, deliver the package, and come home. The men loaded their cargo, prepared their planes, and strapped themselves in. It was the usual crew – Parker, Leo, Lucky, Burke flying alongside the bomber and Hector behind the controls of the bomber itself. Lucky was the last to get in his plane; he stood outside his cockpit, smoking his cigarette to a stump and stomping it out before loading up. His eyes were still cool and calm and there was less of a tremble in his hands.

The ride was long, as usual. The black ocean beneath them welcomed no one and the skies above were ash-grey and dull. The charred Japanese coastline eventually came into view, creeping up slowly on the horizon. Burke echoed the same prayer he made at the chapel to the god above the depths. He wondered if it was even heard. Formation tightened. Reticules set. Ten minutes away from target.

Suddenly, the first ground fire flew past the tip of Burke's wing. A sharp metallic sound signaled, accompanied by sparks. Then the second shot, right in the middle of their formation. Then the third, the fourth, and the fifth shot sounded. All of a sudden, it was bedlam. Ground fire came from all around. The men broke formation frantically, diving and dodging in every direction. They drew up and turned right back down, unleashing a bevy of inaccurate, heavy fire. They could hardly hold on for more than a second. Their radios chimed in: "Stay the course, men!" The ground beneath them lit up in bursts of fire. The accompanying planes scattered, attempting to draw fire away from the bomber. Five minutes away from target. Burke lurched up on the controls of his plane and gained altitude, sweeping from side to side as bullets went past him in a flurry of heated waves. The other men began chattering over the radio, almost inaudibly. Then, on the distant horizon, Shimizu appeared in Burke's sites. It grew larger and larger as he barreled for the target faster and faster. *I want to go home*, he thought, *I just want to go home today*. Three minutes out. "Stay the course!" shouted the radio. *I want to go home!*

"It's way too hot!" Burked shouted into his radio. "I'm-- We got to pull out!"

"Stay the course," came the reply.

"We got to pull out!"

"Stay with it!"

A bullet grazed the top of his wing. It made a ding so loud it nearly drowned out the sound of his engines. *I want out!* he thought. Another bullet grazed past him – it was more than he could take. He let loose another bevy of fire from his bird onto the ground, turned his plane upwards and made a sharp flip. In his peripherals, he could see the others doing the same as the radio finally conceded: "Get out of there, repeat, get out of there!" Leo and Lucky were already falling in beside Burke and together they made the flip. Parker came in on the other side. Hector was still barreling towards Shimizu.

"One minute out!" Hector replied from the bomber, oblivious to the call.

"Did you not hear? Over. Get the hell out of there!"

"Thirty seconds!"

"Dammit Hector, get out – it's too hot!"

"Bomb's out!"

Hector's bomber let loose its payload; bombs fell weightlessly to the ground below, erupting in a flurry of bright, white fire. Hector flew hard on his flip, dragging his plane around and back into formation. His bombs had landed on the earth beneath him, dead center. "Woohoo!" he screamed. "How's that for getting you going in the morning!?"

Burke's knuckles grew white as they clutched the controls. They had finally gathered back together in tight formation, making a beeline for the shore hoping to get back out into open water. Ground fire finally began to taper off. They all began to ease. "Everyone accounted for?" the radio chimed.

"Where's Parker?" someone chimed back.

Down below them, Parker's plane was teetering towards the ocean. The wings and body had been riddled with bullet holes. Parker's radio came in with harsh static. "Mayday, mayday."

"Get out of there, Parker! Ditch it."

"We're going down…"

"Ditch it!"

"Flyer to eject…"

That was it. The radio silenced. "Parker, are you there, over?" No reply. "Parker? Are you there? Over." Nothing. Burke leaned over his controls and spotted Parker's plane beneath him. It was barreling faster and faster to the shallow waters in front of them. Ground fire mercilessly let go another volley against his plane. One of his engines burst into flames. Then, all at once, the plane seemingly dismantled into bits of burning parts. Parker's plane scattered below them on the dark ocean's surface. The flames of the engine leapt up towards the sky. Parker was gone.

Nobody said a word. The flight back was even longer than the flight out. In the distance, Guadalcanal grew larger. Major Allison stood on the tarmac, awaiting their return; his stern eyes counted the planes – eleven. The major dashed back inside and locked the door behind him.

On the runway, none of the men made eye contact. Lucky sat down on the side of the landing strip and lit up a cigarette. Hector climbed out of the cockpit and smashed his helmet to the ground. Leo emerged slowly out of his cockpit, torn to pieces. Burke just stood there on the runway, staring upwards. The cream-colored clouds merged drearily with the ash grey sky. *If that's what grace does for us*, he figured, *then I'd rather have the luck instead.* The quietness of the sky surrounded him and there was nothing left in his heart to say.

That night, at the bar, there was a moment of ceremonial silence. Hector stood up, said a few words about courage, and sat back down. There was a resounding "cheers" to Parker and to courage. Then it was back to life as usual.

SIX

It was 1976. John Burke was in his hospital room, tied to his bed with a hundred tubes running in and out of his body, taking fluids in and out and every which way. A nurse was at the foot of his bed, writing something down in an unknown tongue for the doctor who would inevitably not look at it when he came to visit. Heart attacks took a long time to recover from, especially so in 1976. In 1998, when John had his second heart attack, things went a little more smoothly. That is, they went about as smooth as a sports car over gravel, but it was a step up. The doctor eventually told him that he would have to change his diet and exercise more. Of course, since a doctor said it, John did the exact opposite.

Burke figured doctors were good at two things: not knowing what the real problem was and whitening their own teeth. Beyond that, Burke didn't feel they were of much use to anyone, anywhere. In the course of his life, Burke had been looked at, treated, and examined by doctors all over the world and never wanted to admit he shook hands with one of them. In the 90's, Burke's second wife came down with a rare form of cancer that put her in and out of the hospital. Time and again, the doctors told them that they weren't sure what was going on. Burke knew what was going on; she had *cancer*. It didn't take a medical school genius to figure that she would have problems with it.

After his second heart attack, Burke's family came to his side at the hospital and begged him to do something about his health. He just smiled and nodded as best he could when hooked up to all of the medical equipment. Inside, he thought it was pretty dumb advice. By that point in his life, he figured he didn't have much more to go anyway; what was the point? Thirteen years later, John figured he might have misjudged his longevity. Of course, he contributed the last thirteen years of his life to cinnamon. He had no intention of dieting after the second heart attack. He certainly wasn't going to start exercising. Somewhere he had read that a teaspoon of cinnamon helped the body do something better somewhere, so he gave it a shot. The truth was, it irritated his family to no end that he didn't do more for his health, which gave him quite a kick to watch. This, of course, was more likely what contributed to his longevity.

That is not to say, though, that John hated medicine. In fact, he loved it. It did wonders for him. Granted, some of the side effects were regrettable. He was once placed on a medication for blood pressure that was particularly disagreeable. His ritualistic visit to the bathroom fifteen times a day often ended in either disaster or disappointment. But whatever the case, the medicine did the trick. He figured it was the greatest thing since sliced bread. A tiny pill did so much – changed his entire body in just a few days. The only thing he had against medication was the idiots who were prescribing it, so Burke just stockpiled everything he was ever given. As he grew older, all he needed to do when he was sick was get out the old, outdated medications in lieu of going to the doctor. This gave him great satisfaction, in part because it meant that he didn't have to go to the doctor and because it irritated his family even more. This also added to his longevity.

His hatred for doctors started October 12, 1943. Of all the dates during the war, that was one that stuck with him the most. It was Columbus Day to most Americans, but that wasn't why he remembered it. Burke remembered October 12, 1943, as the day he thought he was giving birth to a small cow in the latrine. It came suddenly and without warning. He had heard of German blitzkriegs happening in Europe, but that morning he was sure one was happening in his lower colon. At 0300 hours, the emergency alarms inside his body shrieked and woke him right up, and continued unrelenting for days. To add insult to injury, he didn't even have reading material; the only thing available to read was the calendar on the wall across from him, which was clearly marked *"October 12, 1943."*

The men in barracks awoke that morning to a permanently occupied latrine. Some of them attempted to enter and console Burke, whose groans and aches filled them with holy panic, but these men didn't make it very far. There was a mass exodus of men going behind the bushes beside the barracks that morning. Major Allison happened across them and erupted in a tizzy of anger, outraged that his men were acting like animals. They got a stern tongue-lashing and were all threatened with Major Allison's "etiquette training," which caused some of them to crumble into nervous breakdowns. Leo, surprisingly, was the only one who stood up for the men. Leo was the one most nervous about getting any more quality time with Major Allison and so pointed the major in the direction of Burke's occupied latrine. Burke heard Major Allison's boot heels stomping their way through the barracks, right up to the door of the latrine.

"Lieutenant Burke, what in the name of Mother Mary are you doing in there?" he screamed. Burke desperately wanted to respond, but was afraid that if he moved or made any sound at all, it would allow more to come out of him, so he just groaned in humiliation. "Lieutenant Burke – you answer me right now!" he screamed again.

Suddenly, Burke heard the door handle begin to jiggle and move. A pang of terror struck Burke. He liked Major Allison too much to risk his life by allowing him to enter the latrine. Burked strained to warn him, but all he could muster was another pathetic groan. It was too late. The sound of Major Allison's boot heel echoed. "Holy mercy from above!" he shouted. The major reeled back into the hallway and stumbled around for a minute, trying his best not to black out. He called for a medic the second he could breathe deeply enough to speak. The men who followed him into the barracks jumped into motion. There was shouting and hollering. Burke swore he even heard someone shout, "Man down!" at one point. By the time the medics arrived, there was speculation that their camp had been the victim of some sort of chemical warfare; HAZMAT suits were being readied on the other side of the camp.

Somehow Burke managed to make it back to the medical tent. He was doubled over in pain, clutching his stomach. There was nothing left inside his body to get rid of and it felt as though his organs were being turned into a heaping pile of goop. Burke prayed for death, or at least a good shot of morphine. It was a slow morning in the medical tent, so every one of the nurses crowded around him, afraid that at any minute he was going to burst open. "Shouldn't we do something?" one of them asked.

"No, wait for the doctor to arrive," said another.

"But what if he can't wait until then?" someone else pleaded.

A debate broke out among the nurses about what to do with him until the doctor arrived. Eventually, they agreed to get a wet towel to put on the back of his neck; the only sure-fire solution they could come up with. Burke couldn't even feel the tiny, soggy cloth, but the nurses all stood back and gloated about what a help they were.

The doctor finally arrived an hour later despite being woken up especially early that morning to come deal with Burke. The doctor carried with him a thermos of coffee in his hands and was still yawning after being rudely woken up from his peaceful, royal slumber. "Where's the patient?" he barked at the nurses. In unison, they pointed at the table that Burke was barreled over on. The doctor took one look at him and sucked all of the air out of the room at once. He was a fresh, new doctor who had been in Army medicine for little over a full week before seeing Burke. He immediately handed his coffee off to one of the nurses and began dancing around the medical tent looking for a chart or handbook to figure out what to do.

"So, Lieutenant Burke," he nervously chattered. "Uh, how are you feeling?"

Burke managed to collect a few thoughts together for him. "Feel like I'm ready for my Miss America debut, you moron."

"Oh, well, uh, good."

The doctor started pressing on Burke's stomach and all along his sides, asking him if it hurt or caused discomfort. Burke responded with dry heaves when the pain was minimal and responded with screaming followed by cursing when the pain was absolutely unbearable. "I think you need to get some gunk out of your system, Lieutenant," he told Burke. "Nurse, can you fetch me some Ipecac, please?" The nurses all scurried off in a hopeful gallop.

Burke had no idea what Ipecac was. Any attempt to find out what it was from the doctor yielded little to no results. However, after that day, Burke never hung onto a bottle of Ipecac, ever, in his life. The nurses brought down a brown, glass bottle and poured out an oozy, black liquid that resembled something like molasses. "What's this do?" Burke asked the nurses.

"It'll get out whatever's left in there," one of the nurses replied.

Before Burke could tell them he had already emptied everything he could have ever ingested since he was five, the nurses shoved the liquid down his throat and jumped back simultaneously. Burke wondered why they jumped back, but for only a moment. The following series of events happened suddenly, like an out of body experience, but not one that enlightened him to any great truth. It was more like a violent eruption from deep within. And after his Ipecac episode, the nurses pumped him full of painkillers and hoped for the best.

Three days later, Burke didn't have so much coming out of him, but he certainly had pain. The military's groundbreaking shaman came back to check on him and push on his stomach some more. The pain had moved from all over Burke's body to mainly just his stomach and sides. The doctor, strangely, found this to be an improvement; Burke would have argued with the doctor's analysis of the situation but still struggled to talk over the pain. The doctor told Burke he was pretty sure it was Burke's gallbladder and it needed removing. Burke didn't know what a gallbladder was but when asked about the prospect of taking it out, he reluctantly agreed. The doctor assured him that he could live without it. John figured that if the good Lord gave it to him, he would probably want to keep it. It was never polite to throw stuff away that God had gifted you with, even if it was causing you outrageous pain. But as he didn't have the energy to argue, Burke consented. So, with all the grace of a skilled veterinarian, the good doctor removed Burke's gallbladder, pumped him full of more painkillers, and waited another three days to see what happened.

Three days later, the doctor returned to tell John that despite the pain and discomfort he was still feeling, on top of the newly developing rash that had broken out all over his body, the surgery was a success and he would be better in no time. Infuriated, Burke scratched out a few curse words from his sore throat, to which the doctor agreed that Burke needed more painkillers.

This went on for another two full days. Burke's rash grew worse and his body still ached all over. It got to the point that the higher ups were starting to consider quarantine. Investigations were about to ensue and letters to superiors were going to be written. John's little sickness had started getting people's attention. Rumors about the enemy using dirty tactics and nerve agents were spreading. Burke almost bought into them himself. None of the men ever came to visit for fear they would get whatever it was he had. Burke didn't blame them. They knew as well as he did that if they were in his shoes, Burke wouldn't have visited them either. Somebody, though, remembered that Burke had gone to the chapel every once in a while since the bombing attack and sent the Devil Dodger himself to make sure Burke's soul was still intact. The chaplain shot into his room one morning, prayed a prayer of healing (and possibly grieving) over him, wished him luck, and darted out as fast as he darted in.

After two days of this, the witch doctor who had been working on Burke for over a week was joined by another, much more seasoned doctor who had just transferred to Guadalcanal from one of the adjacent Solomon islands. The first doctor briefed the older physicians on Burke's strange case, cautioned that he might need to be quarantined, and led the older man over to Burke's bed. The older doctor took one look at him, looked back at his chart, looked at Burke again, and then turned and decked the first doctor right in the mouth. It turned out that Burke never *really* needed his gallbladder removed in the first place. It turned out that the whole charade started with a bad egg salad from the mess hall that didn't settle well. The rash and pain Burke had been feeling for the whole week was caused by none other than the painkillers the first doctor had been pumping mercilessly into his body.

The new doctor took Burke off the painkillers and within twenty-four hours he was back to normal. The men welcomed Burke back with open arms but everyone in the barracks was still pretty wary about letting him stay in the latrine for very long. Burke made up his mind right there that death in the sky didn't seem so bad. The alternative, it seemed, was dying in the medical tent under the hands of certified morons. From that point on, Burke figured that if something happened in the sky, he didn't want to live to tell about it. If he did live to tell about it, it meant that he would probably have to see a doctor about it first. Seeing a doctor again would have been worse than death.

Of course, as it happened, the God who heard his prayer for luck had other plans for him.

SEVEN

They heard the roar of the planes coming in from miles away. It was no surprise to any of them that they were coming. They had pissed them off bad. The Jarheads who had come in to the Guadalcanal only weeks earlier had been preparing to take the rest of the Solomon Islands and work their way up north until they hit Japan. They were tough as nails and extraordinarily motivated. It took a certain kind of man to stand in the front lines of the Marines, just as it took a certain kind of man to fly a plane for the Air Force. There were two big differences between the Marines and Air Force boys, though. First, the Marines weren't as afraid to get blood on their bayonets as the Air Force boys were. Second, the Marines were far more afraid of heights than Air Force boys were. So a deal was cut. The Marines bloodied their bayonets on the ground as the Air Force dropped the bombs from the sky for them. Needless to say, this alliance meant they got along pretty well and worked together often. This also meant that if the Marines had pissed the enemy off, the enemy was pissed off at the Air Force as well.

As a sort of early Thanksgiving present to the Japanese, the Jarheads gave a pounding to Bougainville, a town on one of the northernmost islands in the Solomons. The place was crawling with Japanese who put up a hell of a fight to stand their ground. The Japs were able to hold on for a couple of weeks, but eventually, Bougainville gave up. The enemy had suffered 223 casualties and 8 POWs who were being transferred the following week to Guadalcanal before getting sent off to some other prison far, far from the islands. They had hacked the enemy off enough that back in mainland Japan, bombers were being prepped to come drop their goods on the American base in Guadalcanal. But, of course, the men there knew this. Everybody knew this. The Japanese weren't exactly secret about it. So, while the Japanese thought the Americans were sitting ducks at the base, the men actually sat twenty miles north from the base, preparing to intercept the Japs before they could do any damage.

John Burke manned his station, next to a manned and primed anti-aircraft cannon. They had three AA's positioned to intercept the first attackers and three more positioned a few miles behind them to pick off anyone who snuck through. Scattered in between were men mounted on .50 caliber machine gun turrets to shred the wings of the birds they spotted flying overhead.

Burke heard the enemy birds growing closer and closer. A scout spotted eleven bombers in total rolling in low in the distance. They were flying their way into a clever trap. Even if they were to make it to the base and drop even one of their bombs, there would be no causalities for the U.S. troops. The base had been evacuated and everyone moved a safe distance away. It was the only time Burke had confidence in a strategic plan to fight the enemy and do it relatively safely. The plan was so well laid out and thought through that it was almost menacing watching the enemy buzz their way into their trap.

The enemy fighters hit the beach. They had ten, maybe twelve seconds of flight time before the defenses on the ground let loose. All three front AAs fired almost simultaneously. Two hit their targets directly. The planes burst into balls of fire and scattered to the earth below. The men manning the AA gun near Burke began reloading another shell. Behind them, the first group of machine gunners opened fire. They shredded three more enemy planes that went down on either side of them. It was then that the enemy began dodging and attempting to maneuver around the ground fire. It took Burke's AA cannon a minute longer to line up its sights. They fired. The blast of the cannon pushed Burke back and nearly to the ground; he could feel a peripheral wave of the explosion blow up against him. Another direct hit. Behind him, the rear AA cannons began to fire. They hit another two. The birds left in the sky were flying sporadically. One made a wild beeline to the base while the other two made clumsy evasive maneuvers that began to look like they were about to drop their load on the men below. After reloading their AA cannon for a third time, Burke and the other ground men struggled to line up another shot. They fired again. No good. Another AA cannon to the west of them fired and hit their target, which lit up in a brilliant ball of white fire. Machine gunners in the south, closest to the base, raked holes through the bird that made the beeline. The sound of flying shrapnel rang loudly as the wings of the plane were loaded with holes like Swiss cheese.

One enemy bird was left in the sky. He had had enough and decided to make a flip, aiming his bird back to the north. Somewhere during the flip, his left wing sustained damage and he began losing altitude quickly. Burke could tell the pilot was trying frantically to keep the nose up and to regain altitude, but it was obvious from the ground that he had lost an engine. The bomber plummeted his plane into the ocean, creating an incredible splash of frothy, dark waves. Nobody came out of the hatch. Burk stood on the shore, alongside the other men, waiting for somebody to emerge. Navy boys were already jumping into action like the Marx brothers, riding out in smaller boats to see if the pilot made it. The men behind Burke began packing up their things and getting onto the men standing around, telling them to get back to base. Burke just stood there, looking out at that plane waiting for somebody to come out. If the pilot was still alive in the cockpit, and there was a good chance he was, he must not want to stay alive much longer. Burke imagined him sitting in the cockpit, facing a wall of water on the other side of his windshield and thinking to himself that he could either choose to live with dishonor or die in disgrace of failure. He had only seconds to make that decision – a decision that the ground forces forced upon him. War was cruel like that. Somebody behind Burke suddenly spurred him into action. "Come on, soldier, get moving!" they shouted. Burke turned reluctantly back to base, wishing he could stay and find out what the pilot chose.

As they drove back to base, Burke and the other men passed by some of the wreckage. The birds they had shot out of the sky had been reduced to crumpled piles of burning ash and twisted metal. Some of them were still recognizable. Others were impossible to identify as ever having been a plane. The pilot that had made a beeline for the base had made it closest. His plane, ironically, had sustained the least amount of damage, with just frayed bullet holes from the machine gunners and a sullied belly from the harsh landing. Some of the men went over to see if the pilot had made it through the wreck. Burke looked inside the window of the plane as they drove by. Inside, a silhouette slouched clumsily behind the controls; it had no definite shape or outline, just dead and limp. Burke thought to himself that whatever it was, it was no more.

The men arrived at base at 1600 hours. The first person to greet the men was the chaplain, who said nothing to them as they pulled in. He stood there, solemnly, counting the number of heads that were returning. Lucky, who was sitting beside Burke on the drive back, just shook his head as they passed by. "Guy always gives me the creeps," he groaned.

"Why's that?" asked Leo, chirpily.

Lucky just shook his head.

"I need a beer," said Hector.

"You never go for beers anymore," Burke told him.

"Yeah, well, now's I feel like a beer. It's on me, eh?"

"Really?" Leo asked him.

"Yeah really. It's a good day, ya know. We should celebrate, or something." The other three looked at each other, suspicious of Hector's motives, but conceded that it was indeed a good day. They had all lived another day. That deserved a toast.

That evening, all four of the men joined together for a round of beers at the bar. The bar was filled with soldiers of every kind, as usual. All of the patrons were in varying degrees of drunkenness when they had arrived, also as usual. In fact, everything was normal about that night except that Hector was smiling. It had been the first and only time that any of the men recalled ever seeing Hector smile without having to beat someone up or getting in a drunk altercation of some kind. "Dus' Hector seem kinda strange to ya?" Leo asked Burke.

Burke nodded. "But, free beer," he told him. It could never have been all that bad if Hector was willing to pay for the beer.

That night, the four of them drank three full rounds, all on Hector. It was more beer than any of them had with Hector in weeks. Every now and again, Hector joined the others on the weekends to have one beer or sip on scotch. The problem was that every time any of them took Hector to the bar, he would end up getting in a fight with someone, or even some*thing*. He had once become so angry at a cue stick during a game of billiards that he broke it across a stool next to some poor, unsuspecting private first class. The poor kid nearly peed himself. So eventually, the other three just stopped taking Hector to the bar altogether. The only time he was somewhat pleasant to be around was after they had completed a mission, and usually nobody else was in the mood to be around him then. But, for some reason, on that night Hector wasn't just pleasant, he was calm. And happy. And non-violent. It was incredibly strange to the others. Finally, one of them spoke up.

"What's going on here?" Lucky asked Hector.

"What are ya talking about?" Hector replied.

"What's with the beer, and the singing and being happy and all this crap?"

"Can't a guy have good time now and then, eh?" he pleaded. "Can't I treat my friends to something nice to show a little appreciation to them, now and again?"

"No," Lucky began. "This isn't just having a few beers with friends. This is something else. What is it?"

"It's just a good day, that's all…" Hector pleaded.

"I agree with Lucky," Burke chimed in. "This isn't you, what's different about you today?"

"Hector, what is it!?" Lucky shot back.

Hector crossed his arms, clearly irritated. This was usually where Hector started beating people up. Instead, a smile spread across his face. "Alright, fine, you win," he said. "My son took his first steps today! Well not literally today, but I got the letter today, that he took his first steps! Isn't that something!?"

"You 'ave a son?" Leo asked Hector.

"Of course I have a son."

"Why didn't you say anything before?" Burke asked.

"What? I thought you knew! Isn't it great though?" Hector pulled out a tattered, wallet-sized picture from his inside pocket. "There he is, name's Alfonso Michael Barzini. Cutest little guy on the planet, right?"

"How old is he now?" Lucky asked him.

"Fifteen months now," Hector replied. "I haven't seen him yet. Not in person, anyways. But hopefully I'll get to soon. Very soon."

It was strange how Hector smiled at the picture. It was the only thing besides fighting that any of the men ever saw Hector really smile at. They sat there, watching Hector adore his little boy with all the affection the world could afford to lend him. It changed Hector to even look at his boy. For the others, it was the only time since they had arrived on the front that they enjoyed something out of the sheer pleasure of its goodness. It was a nice change of scenery from the usual.

Burke finally stood up and raised his bottle high. "To Hector. May you be blessed and may your kid live a long and healthy life."

"To Hector," the others resounded.

It was the first time Burke had ever given a toast. It was also the first time any of the men in the bar gave a toast for something other than the fallen or for not dying themselves. On nearly every face willing to concede to sympathy crept a small but meaningful smile of endearment.

The men drank one more round, got just drunk enough to have a good time but not regret it later, and stumbled their way back to the barracks. It was a quiet night, very still and frosty cold. Even the usual chatter of the other soldiers moseying their way back home after a long night of drinking was calmer than usual. The only light visible to the four was in front of them, a dull light from a mobile lantern near the barracks. As they neared it, they discovered temporary cells had been created where the prisoners from Bougainville would stay. They were dimly lit and dank in appearance. It was the first time any of the men had seen the cells being used. As the four came even closer, they could make out the dull commotion of the soldiers getting the prisoners into the cells. Burke watched inquisitively; he wished deep down that he had not. The prisoners were thin and pale, walking skeletons with the waning glow of a soul. Their bodies were frail, broken, and riddled. One of them had a noticeable limp in a leg that appeared twisted and cracked. The man's cheeks were concave, covered in about a week's worth of scruff trailing up to the north of his upper lip. The prisoners' clothes were plain, grey, torn. But it wasn't their appearance that bothered Burke inside. It was their eyes. There was an immense amount of pain, brokenness, and dishonor in the depths of their eyes that haunted Burke for the rest of his life. Those glazed, charcoal pupils and bloodshot whites – they were nearly sucked of all light left in them.

As the four of them walked past, one of the prisoners caught Burke's eyes with his directly. The prisoner's eyes were so dark and cold that Burke couldn't tell his pupil from his irises. The man's face made no expression and neither did his body. In the deep, frigid stare of the prisoner, Burke saw the pilot in the water from earlier that day.

He thought of the tenacity of the pilot, to commit to his bird all the way to the ocean. If the pilot had survived, he'd have nothing but dishonor to live with. That was exactly what Burke saw in the prisoner's eyes – disgrace and dishonor. Burke wondered what it took to go down with the ship like that.

None of the four of them said a word about the prisoners that night. In fact, none of them spoke of the prisoners or ever made a reference to them. However, they were all very aware of the prisoners' presence among them. As Burke went to sleep that night, his mind spun circles around the downed pilot in the ocean. *If it were me,* he thought to himself, *which would I choose?* He couldn't make up his mind and was never really sure. Eventually, he could scarcely decide whether each day was worth living through or not, and it never got easier to decide.

EIGHT

Burke stood at the top of the sharp outset over the murky waters below him, stark naked. The air was colder than the devil's soul; shivers quaked his body so hard that he nearly believed his organs were shivering too. The waters far below gave him no warm welcome. Trembling, Burke took a step forward and felt the moss between his toes squish slimily as he dug his feet into the ground. It was Thanksgiving, 1943.

Burke never really celebrated Thanksgiving. Once, years before, when his father was still around, his family had a traditional turkey dinner. However, the civility around the table lasted only as long as his father's drinking habit could hold out. Around the country that year, people were celebrating Thanksgiving with turkey, stuffing, and mashed potatoes, gathering around a table with their favorite family members and swapping stories of the better days they had. Back at base, some of the soldiers gathered around the mess hall tables and cracked dirty jokes with fellow soldiers, telling stories of better years that never actually happened. There was a small group of men who decided to "carve" pumpkins they stole from the mess hall with their M1 Garands, telling stories of better years that had yet to come. Burke, Leo, Lucky, and Hector, however, decided on a whim that they needed to seize the day before them and be thankful for the year they were in. Leo nervously assured the others that they all had plenty of adventure to be thankful for in the first place, rightfully afraid that if they got a wild hair to do something adventurous, one of them would end up in the medical tent.

"...jus' think of the other day when we alls went fishin', sittin' *quietly*, enjoyin' the day and all..." he urged the others. The other three thanked him for reminding them of the little things in life to be grateful for, and for reminding them about the fishing hole. So, with beer and carved turkey in tow, the four headed down to the fishing hole to do some "fishing."

It wasn't until they got there that Leo questioned them about not taking fishing poles. "Who needs a stupid fishing pole," Hector asked him, "when you can go down there and get them yourself?" Hector cackled madly. Leo cowered and scolded himself for his lack of foresight. Lucky was already halfway undressed.

Everybody but Leo was ready to make the leap of faith off the cliff and into the grimy, sludgy pond below. That is, everybody was ready right up until they were about to do it. The men stood on the top of the cliff, all stark naked except for Leo who refused to shed his clothes for what they were about to do. They all looked down at the water like a bunch of idiots looking at a disaster waiting to happen. Leo wanted to chime in an "I told ya so!" but had a hard time getting it past the chattering of his teeth. Burke and Hector, shivering their brains out of their head, turned to Lucky for consultation. Lucky stood there as still as a statue, completely unfazed. Lucky was possibly the hairiest man any of them had ever seen. The others wondered if, with all of his natural insulation, Lucky shouldn't have been sent to the European front. He was probably the only American who had enough hair to keep him warm enough to fight the Ruskies during a Russian winter. They figured he'd probably outlive the Russians themselves. Naturally, they figured Lucky should be the first to jump and offered him front and center. Lucky smirked at their childish offer and responded by sitting down on a rock, lighting a cigarette, and puffing away stubbornly.

One of them eventually suggested drawing lots to see who would go first. They all drew. Burke came up short. The others gave him the kind of stare one would give a dog right before the dog is sent off to be neutered. Sympathy mixed with apathy and a dash of "glad it wasn't me" for good measure.

Burke turned solemnly, unwilling to accept his dire fate. It was a mere fifteen-foot drop but from his vantage point, Burke figured it was an all-out, ten-second free-fall. "There is no way that I am doing this by myself," he shivered.

"Come on ya pansy," Hector said, encouragingly. "Don't be a wimp."

"No, not a chance," he replied. Burke had no intention of going out like this.

"Leo, go help him out," Hector ordered.

"No sir," Leo replied. "I din't even wanna come out here an' do this cotton'-pickin' thing in the first place."

"Why don't you jump with him?" Lucky offered Hector. Hector started to shoot back a halfway valid excuse, but realized that excuses for this sort of adventure were less valid when one was already stripped down to their skivvies. "Come on," Lucky said. "Be brave, huh? Do it."

Hector glared back at Lucky viciously. "Fine," he said, puffing out his chest deliberately. Hector came up beside Burke along the side of the cliff and joined him in looking down at the water below. The longer they looked at it, the further away it seemed to be. Hector found himself unable to look away from the surface of the water, as if it had cast a magical spell on him and turned him to stone. Slowly, Hector's look of bravery turned to concern. Hector and Burke begrudgingly edged their way closer to the drop, as if waiting for the other to jump first.

"Oh, come on, jump!" Lucky shouted behind them. Burke and Hector just stood there defiantly. "Jump!" No jumping. "Gah, fine, I'll help you jump," Lucky grumbled as he flicked out his cigarette and began marching towards them. That became motivation enough for Burke and Hector to go; their fear of Lucky was far greater than their fear of any pond in all of the Solomon's. With a leap, Hector and Burke plummeted to the grungy water below. The cold air sucked the voice from their throats, constricting their windpipes like an anaconda.

Their feet touched the surface of the water and instantly turned them to ice. Luckily, the blood in their veins designed to maintain the body temperature kept the rest of their bodies from totally freezing. However, one "appendage" in particular had the unpleasant misfortune of hitting the ice-cold water, without the protection of any warm blood flow. Burke was particularly afraid that it had come flying off on impact. The rest of their bodies continued to submerge in suit. As soon as they were completely submerged, both Burke and Hector immediately wanted to shoot back up, as if in revolt against the cold water. When they had bobbed back up to the surface, they quickly whipped their heads wildly to find a way out of the water. Hector spotted a landing and motioned emphatically for Burke to follow.

From above, Burke and Hector heard their cohorts hollering and hooting. They weren't cheering. They were indeed oo'ing and ah'ing, but not because they were impressed. It was a painful sort of "oo…" that chimed as they emerged from the water onto the shore. This worried Hector and Burke quite a lot. Leo came stumbling down the hillside, tripping over Hector and Burke's clothes that flew clumsily out of his hands. "Y'all okay!? Holy cow!"

"Yeah, we're fine Leo," John assured him.

"No, you're not," said the hairy Big Foot marching down the hillside, sucking on a fresh new cigarette.

"What are ya talking about?" Hector asked Lucky.

"Look," Lucky told him. They did. All along their bodies, covered from head to toe, were little black, tube-like creatures.

"What the hell are those things?" Hector shouted.

Lucky began to let go of a deep laugh. That made Hector and Burke feel even worse about their circumstance. Laughter meant that Lucky knew something they didn't and that he was glad it wasn't him. Leo edged in closer to Hector and Burke, who were rolling around on the shore, frantically trying to get black creatures off. Leo stayed a safe distance away from the men, as if one of the black tubes would jump on him. "Oh, I know what them's are; them's are *leechees*."

"What!?" Burke asked him.

"Leeches," Lucky said in between chuckles. "You are covered in leeches!"

Hector and Burke panicked. They darted up and began tugging harder at the creatures covering their bodies. "There ain't no use in doin' that," Leo cautioned them. "Them creatures don't come off for just about anythin'!" This, of course, comforted the men ever more.

"Well what are we supposed to do!?" screamed Hector.

"I bet Major Allison could help you out," Lucky laughed as he began to dress himself.

"Ha, ha! Very funny, smart guy," Hector replied.

"Come on, what are we going to do!?" John begged.

"I got an idea," Leo suggested. "We used to git' these little guys on us all the time back home. We used to burn 'em off."

"Burn!?" Burke yelled.

"Alright, alright, we got another way. Come on," Leo said, motioning for them to follow.

Leo led them back to the outskirts of base, stopping so that they would remain unseen from the men in the camp. Hector and Burke were still naked and sopping wet. Lucky was still getting dressed and still laughing at their expense. Hector threatened him at one point, but this only made Lucky laugh harder. Suddenly, Leo spotted the large metal drum he was searching for and told the others to stay put as he fetched it for them.

"Now, this'll probably hurt like hell," he told them, struggling to move the barrel over to them. "Like I's said, we usually burned them off, but of course we never had so many of 'em on us at one time back home! I'm sure this'll do the trick."

Leo strained to open the top of the drum. "What's in there?" Burked asked him, wearily. Then they smelled it. Gasoline. Fifty-gallons worth.

"Sorry, fellas, it's the best I's got."

"No way! I'm not doing that," Hector bellowed.

"You could always go to the medical tent and get them taken off, one at a time," Lucky suggested. Hector and Burke decided the drum wasn't such a bad idea. Leo and Lucky helped the men get positioned over the barrel, one at a time. The gasoline looked much worse to them than the sludge back at the pond. "Quicker the better, boys," Lucky advised them. Neither of the men spent more than even five seconds in the drum each. It felt as if someone had set an oil fire to the surface of their skin. They both screamed so high and so loud, some of the men in the base thought there was another chimpanzee infestation. When Hector and Burke had emerged, there were only a few of the buggers left. Leo, unwittingly, had the bright idea of taking a match and burning off what had remained. Lucky ardently advised him to wait until after they had washed off the gasoline from their bodies. Burke and Hector were grateful that Leo agreed.

The next day, all four men were called into briefing at 0700 hours. Major Allison was giving the updates on activities in the Pacific. While he was lecturing about a Naval escapade happening that day between Buka and New Ireland, the major stopped dead in his tracks. He squinted to the back of the room where Hector and Burke were trying to stay unseen. "Lieutenant Burke and Lieutenant Barzini, look up! What's on your faces?"

"Ah crap," Hector whispered under his breath. Somewhere in the room, they could hear Lucky still giggling like a little girl.

"Lieutenants," Major Allison shouted, "show me your faces."

They complied. Covering their bodies, from head to toe, were tiny, delicate hickey marks and burns left by the leeches and gasoline the day before. It was anything but pretty.

"What in the name of Sam Hill did you two do?" the major barked.

"We found some leeches, sir," Burke replied.

The major shook his head. "And why were you looking for leeches, boys? Did you think you were going to eat them?"

"It seemed like a good idea at the time, sir," Hector piped in. The major didn't like that response very much.

"Then why does it look like someone lit you boys on fire?" he asked.

"We got them off with gasoline, sir," Burke told him.

"You did what!?"

"Seemed like a good idea at the time, sir," Hector added again. The major liked that response even less the second time.

"You boys better see me after briefing," he ordered them.

They waited until the other men had left. Burke and Hector were far more afraid of what Major Allison was going to do to them than they had been about jumping into the pond. The men stood at attention as the major glared at the two of them, fiercely. He ordered them to tell him the story, the whole story from start to finish, and they did, delicately leaving out the part that Leo and Lucky were with them (this was, of course, in good taste and manners).

"That was stupid," the major reminded them. They already knew, in retrospect of course. "So stupid in fact, that dipping yourself in gasoline was punishment enough. So I'm not going to even punish you for being *morons*. But you do owe me for the barrel of gas you two dingbats sullied. I'm putting you both on an extra patrol shift this week. You can pay me back for the gas by doing some actual work."

It could have been worse. Much worse. Staying awake until 0200 hours for a double shift of patrols wasn't bad, considering. Hector and Burke moseyed their way out to the edge of the base, loaded and geared up. For Hector, it was almost a blessing. He got to stay up all night and carry a gun around more than usual, the kind of thing that would typically put him in a good mood. The patrol was also usually pretty easy. Guadalcanal was not the kind of place that attracted a lot of ground resistance. The Japs had a hard enough time standing their ground where they were, so they rarely had the chance to come knocking on the Allies' door in Guadalcanal.

That night had been quiet, as usual. Hector and Burke kept their eyes open, but never had any reason to expect any excitement. The men made their rounds and were mostly silent, making conversation here and there when they had a trivial fact to bring up. It was the most, in fact, Burke had ever talked to Hector, though. Hector was never the kind of guy someone felt they could walk up to and start talking with. At about 0130, though, Burke's eyes began to betray him. They began to sink lower and lower, feeling heavier and heavier. He tried to wake himself up, slapping his face and shaking his head from time to time, which did not prove effective. Since conversation had been keeping him awake most of the night, he turned to Hector: "You ready to get back to your family?" Burke asked him.

"Yeah, who isn't, right?"

"Sorry, just trying to stay awake," Burke admitted, pointing to his dreary eyes.

"Nah, don't worry about it. You know, some guys don't like questions like that. But I couldn't honestly give a care. But yeah, I miss 'em. Want to see my kid someday. That would be nice."

"I understand."

"What about you?" he asked.

"Me?" Burke cocked his head. Hector's question made him instantly think of his mother. John had only written two letters while he was away, both to his mother. The first, she didn't respond to. After the second one, she sent back a drunken, poorly scrawled piece of paper, belittling the military and telling him that the president was a moron, and so on. Burke could tell she was drunk when she wrote it. She hardly did anything sober. She concluded her letter with the words, "Don't die. —Mom" After that, Burke decided to never write her again; she had said all that was really on her mind to say, anyways. Burke looked at Hector and replied, "I don't know. Maybe." It was the only thing he felt he could say without being disrespectful to his mother. She might have been a drunk, and a terror, but Burke always had a respect for her somewhere within him. She was a tough old broad.

"Yeah, I understand," said Hector. "Don't like talking about family. Some guys are like that." By "some guys are like that," Hector really meant that for some guys, the war wasn't all that bad when compared to the nightmare back home. For some men, for men like Burke, war was a vacation from something worse.

"Well I hope you get to see your son very soon," Burke told Hector quickly, attempting to move the conversation back to him.

"Yeah, thanks. Figure the harder I fight here, the faster we can get this war over with and I can see his face, right?"

"Yeah."

Suddenly, off in the thicket in front of them, the sound of a tree branch cracked loudly and gave way to something in it. Burke and Hector both shot up, trying to see what it was through the branches of the trees. Hector thought he saw a shadow move, and then became sure of it. "You see that?" he whispered to Burke. They squinted through the darkness; Burke could make out the soft, hazy outline of a person, standing up from the ground where the branch had snapped. Hector motioned for them to creep up closer on it. Staying low, they hugged the ground as close as they could with their knees. Another branch gave way to the north. Leaves rustled. Twigs burst. The person in the darkness stopped.

The sights of their weapons made a cold, straight line from their eyes to the barrel of their muzzles, trained into the abysmal darkness. Hector motioned for the two of them to split as he broke away to one side. Burke made a wide turn to the west, deciding to go out far and come up behind the person. Hector disappeared out of sight to the east. All of a sudden, the shadowman darted down low and shot across the ground. He had taken off, running.

Burke and Hector took off in a sprint right behind him. The shadowman's frantic run gave way to snapping twigs and flying branches to the north. To the east, Burke could hear Hector furiously dodge tree limbs and brushes, closing in as fast as he could. He had managed to make it in front and to the right of Burke by about fifty meters. It was then that the shadowman began veering west, heading right towards Burke. Burke zeroed in, trying to get closer to him so he could make a tackle. The creature quickly leaped clear over his head and into a nearby tree, climbing it frantically and quickly. It was then that Burke noticed the creature's tail whip the leaves around it and it climbed faster and faster. Burke's sprint turned into a jog, which turned into a pace. It was a waste of time, nerves that had gotten the better of them – nothing to worry about at all. A smile nearly crept up on Burke's face just thinking about it.

"Hector, I think we're fine—"

Suddenly, there was a flare of light. It was bright, incredibly bright. A fierce blast accompanied the flare not even a second later, coming from Burke's right. Small trees and underbrush scattered wildly about. In the west, a small grey cloud of smoke plumed, carrying itself around trees and shrubs like a thick fog. Burke took off in a quick bolt towards the site. There was nothing left. Not a thing. The ground was leveled, emptied. Burke searched frantically. The blood pumping from his heart pounded in his ears. The smoke from the blast filled his lungs with more and more panic. It was then that Burke spotted him.

Hector was face down in the bushes, on the edge of the blast radius. There was virtually nothing left where his left foot should have been except mangled flesh. Hector's standard issue rifle laid nearly twenty feet from where he was, charred and blackened by the explosion. Burke dropped his weapon and slipped over to Hector. Upon closer inspection, Hector's diaphragm was still moving, but only slightly. Burke grabbed him and flipped him over quickly, but gently.

Blood covered his whole face; his nose was mangled and crushed. The tops of his eyelids fluttered aimlessly as he struggled to open them. Burke, however, only noticed how bad Hector's left foot had looked and thought how badly he needed a tourniquet. Hector suddenly grabbed at Burke's lapel and face, frightened nearly to death. With one hand, Burke pushed him back down and with the other hand reached for his gear. Burke was screaming, begging for help. Engines to the south of the men rumbled lowly and dim headlights beamed towards them through the trees and smoke. From his bag, Burke brought out a tourniquet and slipped it on over Hector's left leg. It squeezed tight over Hector's knees and Hector let out a yelp of pain. As the headlights got closer, Hector flung his arms at Burke's lapel again. He tried to bring him in closer, saying something almost inaudibly about his son. Burke held him down to the ground, trying to keep him still, and shushed him gently and calmly. A drop of water fell and hit Hector's charred chest; Burke reached up to his cheek — it was his own tears.

A jeep flung dirt all about as it pulled up beside them. Soldiers fell out of the vehicles, some with their weapons drawn and ready while others ran and immediately started strapping Hector onto a board. It was utter chaos. Hector laid there while the men did their work, blood dripping down his face and legs. Orders were being shot back and forth between the men and some of them pointed at each other and yelled even louder in panic. They managed to strap Hector in and loaded him into the jeep. The jeep took off and Burke stood there, watching the men take his friend back to base, and eventually disappear from sight.

Burke stood motionless, a small man in the midst of all the tall trees and overgrowth. Somewhere, way off in the distance, a monkey cackled madly from a treetop. Burke flung around towards the noise furiously: "Dammit, you! Screw you! Dammit — you bastard, you stupid bastard! Go die you damn animal, go and die you son of a bitch!—ah, God!" Burke fell to his knees, weeping. He thought about where Hector was going, where he was being taken, and if he himself would ever go there as well to see Hector again. Burke wept harder.

None of the other men ever saw Hector again. Toasts were made in his honor and nights even passed by without sleep for some of the men. The bar became much quieter and far more lonely without him there. The others never spoke of Hector to each other, but each knew deep down what the other felt about the situation. It was quiet. And that was the absolute worst.

It was years later that Hector reemerged - long after the war. Burke was living in New Mexico with his first wife and first two kids. Somehow Hector managed to find him and write a letter; he filled him in on what happened the rest of that night. Hector had stepped on a landmine that had gone overlooked in initial sweeps, one that luckily had been miswired and had a delay in the switch. If he had not been sprinting, it would have taken more than his left foot. The soldiers drove him back to the medical tent where, after hours of cleaning and medicating, the doctor amputated what remained of his left foot and then shipped him off to the mainland. One month later, Hector saw his son's face for the first time. The letter touched Burke's old heart. They wrote a few more times back and forth to each other and eventually Burke asked Hector to send a photo of himself.

After the war, Burke could only remember what Hector had looked like from the image of seeing Hector's bloodied face as they loaded him onto the stretcher. As if the war was not bad enough, *thinking* about the war was far worse. Trying to get that image out of his head was one of the hardest things Burke had to do after the war. Finally one Christmas, after they had been mailing each other for some time, Burke got a letter with a picture in it. It was Hector, standing on his last leg, with his son dressed in cap and gown. Their smiles went from ear to ear. From that day on, Burke never again thought of Hector on that stretcher. *Hector was a lucky son-of-a-gun,* Burke thought to himself, smiling. He was right. That is the cruelty of war – misfortune is sometimes the only thing that will save your life.

NINE

December of 1943 was a month of the war few forgot, including Lieutenant John Burke. It was a tough year for Americans all around. A lot of people watched a lot of death and destruction happen, for the first time, from the comfort of their own homes or movie theatres. News anchors started showing up on bases across almost every front, including Guadalcanal. At first, a lot of the men didn't think the news reporters were worth their weight in manure. They came out with the cameras, tripods, combed hair, and flak jackets and made sure to record every scene they could from every angle they could, even if it was absolutely insane to do so. At first, the men figured the anchors would just sit back and watch the war unfold from the safety of the big guns – they were surprised that they didn't. The anchors edged their way to the front lines and shot everything they saw. Back home on the mainland, people were feeling, for the first time, only a dose of what the men were feeling on the front lines for the first time. Some called it a "call to arms." One anchor even called the war "Orchestrated Hell." Burke always thought that title was the most fitting. It didn't quite show the whole picture, but it at least was close enough to give an idea of war. People watching on the television back on the mainland could see a glimpse of what the U.S. forces were doing on the front lines, which made things not so distant anymore. It was an uncomfortable feeling – seeing brothers, fathers, dying on national news. It made a lot of people get up and get out of their homes and do something to help the war efforts. It also made December 1943 a long winter for everybody.

At the time, all eyes were on the European front. People on the mainland saw pictures of Berlin and London up in smoke and thought, for a while anyway, that hell was localized to only the Europeans. A lot of people forgot about Japan. Burke, for one, didn't blame them for neglecting the Pacific front. It was hard to see what was happening in the Pacific when all eyes were turned in a different direction. But things in the Pacific were not much different. It was not as cold as the European front, but they were really no different. Bombing raids continued almost daily, Jarheads marched their way on through the beaches and shores of the Solomon Islands, and the Navy was still floating around on the black waters blowing anything out of the sky that flew over them. The men on the base were a little less jovial than usual, though. For most of them, December meant Christmas, and that meant tradition and family. It was the first Christmas most of them had spent away from family, especially that far away. There were no traditions to be had on base, either, and nobody wanted to start any. Deep down the men figured that if they started a tradition, that would suggest that they would be there the next year to do it again, which was something none of them wanted. Needless to say, none of the men felt much like celebrating the spirit of Christmas.

It was the night right before the men were slated for a bombing run to Fukuoka, a city smack dab between Hiroshima and Nagasaki. It was nothing special – dive bomb the city until they could find nothing left to bomb – and it was not supposed to be anything special. Lucky, Leo, and Burke were out having a beer as they usually did before a run. Ever since Hector had gone, none of them said much to each other. When Leo and Lucky had caught wind that Hector was taken away the night of the blast, Leo immediately broke down into a sobbing mess. Lucky didn't say a word; he stood in the barracks, looking at the ground with the white of his knuckles growing stronger and more intense on his balled-up fists. It had been two weeks since Hector had stepped on the mine. Two weeks of saying nothing to each other, minus the occasional grunt or nod of affirmation. Finally, after two weeks, Leo broke the silence.

"I miss Parker," he said wearily.

"Shut up, Leo," Lucky shot back.

"I do, I miss 'im," Leo replied.

"You shut up right now," Lucky said as he lunged at him across the table.

"Why? Why should I not say sumthin' about how I's feel? I miss 'im all! Alright, so there."

Lucky jumped from his chair and started around the table

towards Leo. Burke intercepted him, halfway falling out of his chair. "Let it be," Burke pleaded.

Lucky pushed him to the ground. "Stay out of my way, John, and you – shut up! I'm sick of hearing that line of crap. I don't want to hear it alright?"

"I can say what I want to!" Leo interjected.

"Leo, don't," Burke urged him.

"You have something to say?" Lucky shot back. "Fine, say it. Make your peace. You want to say a few words, clear your conscious, go ahead. Be my guest."

"Yeah, I do. And I will!" Leo said with a burst of courage. He stood up and started towards Lucky, cautious of his own bravery. He stopped before getting too far, realizing it was a bad idea. "I miss Parker. I wish he din't die. He was a good kid, a God-fearin' kid. What'd he ever do to them, er anybody for that matter."

Lucky chimed in. "You think God-fearing is enough to merit you life? You think *God* is going to keep you alive? You think he cares? Listen you little snot-nosed bastard, God doesn't care about you, or me, whether we live or die. He is just watching us tear each other to pieces. God isn't the one you should be fearing, it's the bastards who are trying to shoot you out of the sky! It's the cowards back home waiting to greet you with disappointment and rejection, who think you're nothing but a blood lusty monster. It's the guy who'll smash a bottle across your face just for asking him if he's doing alright – the drunks who don't give a rat's ass about you because you're nothing more than the bastard son of a bad idea."

Lucky stopped. Leo and Burke were both looking back at him with eyes the size of saucers. He shook his head and touched his face. Tears were falling across his cheeks, making crooked pathways, following the patterns of his bottle-shaped scars. He inspected the liquid he wiped from his face curiously and then looked at the others. They said nothing.

Lucky sank back down into his chair and pulled a cigarette from his pocket. His hand was trembling; he could hardly hold a match up to light the cigarette. Leo turned to Burke and asked him if they should do something. Burke motioned for him to say nothing. They all gathered themselves back into their chairs slowly. Not a word was spoken the rest of that evening. After a time, they finished their beers and went to bed.

The next morning was especially cool. There was a coastal breeze that made everything smell like salty water and stung everybody's lungs. The breeze that morning was soulless and dark, which made a chilling cold creep up Burke's spine and made him shake all over. It started in his shoulders and radiated out across his arms and up through his neck, making each hair stand on end at attention. The men stood in the open tent, waiting in exhaustion for briefing to begin. Major Allison entered quickly and immediately began going over the flight plan and mission details. According to their intelligence, their flight path should have bypassed the enemy's anti-aircraft defenses and given them a clear shot in and out of Fukuoka. It *should* have, at least. They were going to go out wide around and behind the island, approaching the enemy from the rear.

It would add an hour to their flight plan, but it was worth it to avoid getting blown out of the sky. Major Allison finished the briefing and they were loading up by 0730. The major appeared especially tired that morning.

The men loaded their things into their aircraft. Not a word was spoken. It was a small group of dive bombers, six in total. When briefing had ended, Lucky had darted out in front of the other men and immediately jumped into his plane. As the others loaded, he was already in his cockpit, waiting nervously for everyone else to go up. Burke loaded his gear and strapped on his helmet, the cold shiver still quaking his body all over. As he climbed into his cockpit, he pulled out his Bible just far enough from his jacket pocket to kiss it and put it back, as had been his habit for some time. Leo was the only one of them wanting to say anything. He nervously looked over at Burke, began to open his mouth, but refrained as nothing came out.

The air was choppy that morning. Turbulence jostled the men around every twenty seconds. The men flew especially high so that the island came into view much earlier than usual. The island was still ashy grey and smoldering, just like they had left it. Below, the water seemed to extend forever in every direction with no sign of enemy contacts. One of the men commented on the quiet waters over the radio, as if it were a good thing. Burke was the only man flying that morning who found quiet waters more terrifying than busy waters. The water reminded him of the morning Parker's plane went down. Burke thought of him, floating around down in the deep joined by a host of other good men who had gone before him, men who'd fallen from good graces with God. Somehow that morning, strange as it was, the sky was blue, a bright blue that reflected off the ocean, as if smiling on the men below. Suddenly, Burke found himself whispering a prayer he had heard the kid Parker say long before. He found himself asking for mercy, not luck, this time. Luck, he figured, would only let him live longer in hell. Mercy might somehow bail him out of the bondages of war. The god hovering over the void that day was the same god in the depths below. He was the only thing standing between life and death.

"Let's come up around, gentlemen," the radio chirped. "Target, twenty minutes out."

The city eventually came into view, peaceful and strangely untouched. Not a thing stood in the way between the city and the men. They turned the birds out wide in the sky, positioning themselves for Fukuoka and into their flight plan. As they zeroed in, the small town looked more and more peaceful in the reticules. Ten minutes out from target and there was no ground resistance to be seen or heard. Their formation dipped and prepared to drop. Five minutes out, still nothing. They steadied their birds perfectly, only tumbling here and there with turbulence. Two minutes. It was a milk run.

The bombs dropped.

Nothing happened. It was perfect, smoother than any run any of them had made before. Not a peep or chirp from the enemy. Burke breathed a sigh of relief; perhaps the god of the skies and the depths listened. Perhaps he more freely gave out mercy than he did luck. As their load leveled the ground beneath them, whipping up dirt and rubble all around, the thought struck Burke that maybe what he was given wasn't *actually* mercy. The debris from the ground scattered beneath him. Homes, businesses – leveled and demolished. Lives, lost. He never wanted this. How was he any different than his rotten employer, McDuff? *All this damn power and this is what we do with it?* he thought. That's when the call came in to go ahead and pull up, they were going home.

The men made their flip and aimed the noses of their planes back in the same direction they had come from – over the water and out wide around the island. As they made their turn, Burke saw the ocean appear from over the land. It had turned black as coal and full of evil. It was waiting for them. Sitting on the surface of the ocean was the devil himself, waiting to welcome them to the depths with open arms. Three enemy vessels had crept out onto the murky waters. The lead plane quickly considered going back over the island, going home over the south. Behind them, however, were land defenses that rang out their first shot past the wings of the men. Over the radio came the last words Burke ever heard his cohorts report:

"Dear God, help us."

The enemy was attacking, not for protection, but to send them all to the depths of hell.

The lead plane took the first hit from the AA guns to the south. It erupted in a ball of fire and spread chinks of the plane's metal body all across the sea below. The men immediately broke formation. Enemy fire broke all around, creating an inferno of bullets and shrapnel. Burke yanked hard on the controls, cracking his knuckles against the stick, and aimed his plane back towards the city of Fukuoka. Behind him, another plane took a hard hit; half of the plane dissolved in the blast and the other half plummeted to the ground. The coastline was in Burke's sights. *If I can make it to the coast, I could at least get out of the reach of their fire*, Burke thought. It was then that Burke could see Leo's plane coming up alongside him, out of his peripherals. Leo had taken a blow across his left wing. Burke radioed in to Leo.

"Stay level, buddy," he radioed. "Keep her level!" Leo was scared out of his wits, shaking madly and crying as he tried to maintain his plane.

Suddenly, from far behind, Burke heard the fade of an engine wane as it sunk to the surface of the water. The mayday call came through – another bird was down. Burke anxiously radioed in to Lucky, hoping he was still alive.

"Lucky, are you there? Over."

The radio crackled back at him. Nothing.

"Lucky, come in. Over."

Still nothing. All of a sudden, from down below Burke and Leo on the coastline, a volley of machine gun bullets raked across their wings. Leo's fuel tank was hit, hemorrhaging gasoline from its side all over the sky. *We aren't going home*, Burke thought. Deep down, he knew it was true; his heart fell. Both of them were losing altitude quickly and desperately needed to set down. Burke noticed a clearing in the trees several kilometers to their east. He immediately radioed Leo and told him to set down there as they began to plummet to the ground below. A bright smoke started billowing from one of his engines and dissipated all around. One of his engines had been shot, Burke thought. Over the radio, the two heard a call come through. It was Lucky.

"Boys, you still there?"

Burke looked around frantically at the sky for signs of Lucky. "We're falling hard, Lucky. Mayday, mayday."

Burke finally spotted him. Lucky's plane had caught fire and had veered way out over the ocean. The nose of his plane was darting back and forth violently, heading out further into open water. Lucky was falling too, down into the black waters. Between him and waters below sat a Japanese vessel, bulldogging its place in the ocean. There was no doubt it was the one that had put the fatal blow in Lucky's plane. Lucky was nearly fifty meters directly above it, looking straight into its cruel, red eye. The radio static started in again. Burke could only make out two full words.

"...Thank y... God-...-aring gentleme..."

Suddenly, Burke's plane darted underneath the brush of the tree line; he had undershot the clearing by a ways. Branches and leaves whacked the side of his plane and scraped the sides of it, slowing him down. Above him, the roar of Leo's engines blew past him. Leo had at least made it to the clearing, but the smell of fire penetrated Burke's nose. Burke couldn't tell if it was coming from Leo's engines or from his cockpit before the front of Burke's plane hit a tree, unrelenting to his decent. The tail of his bird suspended up in the air and let itself down to the ground below, jolting his head backwards and hitting his head on the back of his seat.

And everything went black.

PART II

ONE

    On the flag that hung above John's dining room table were marks that no one in his family ever noticed or would have noticed. It was, in fact, the only way he truly knew how to identify the flag. Burke didn't read a lick of Japanese, so the scrawled writing on either side of the rising sun could have been changed daily and he would never have known. In fact, the flag had been upside-down for the longest time. It wasn't turned right-side-up until his daughter's hippie boyfriend mentioned it. There was only the one mark on it that Burke ever recognized – hardly noticeable if you weren't shown where it was – and it was the *only* thing it seemed he could ever see. Not even the hippie in his living room said a word about it. The little marks stuck out to John, though, like a sore thumb.

    In the lower left hand corner of the big red circle – the "circle of the sun" as it is called – are three bloody smear marks. They are small and have grown very faint over time. The red of the circle on the flag almost drowned out the marks completely. Nobody had ever noticed them; if they had, they never mentioned it to Burke.

When John's family took the flag to have it framed, he almost died of a stroke. He grew anxious and worried that it would get damaged, or the framers would botch the job up completely. For all he knew, his family had tucked it away in some storage building to give to their grandkids to play with one day and had replaced his flag with a fake that was in better shape, some novelty replica or something. The first thing Burke did when his family showed him the flag, reverently displayed in its frame, was to check the circle of the sun for the bloody smear marks. They were there, of course. It was the first time Burke had actually ever seen the flag spread out like it was. At the most, he used to only check a corner of it as it poked a corner out of its bag while in storage. Burke hardly ever opened the bag completely and looked at the whole thing.

It was also the first time John had ever seen it through glass before. As his family presented him with the framed flag, John looked deep into his reflection, right above the bloody smear marks. During the middle of the night that night, he snuck into the living room where they first had it hung and stared at his reflection in the glass and at the smear marks. Since he was the only one who knew they were there, nobody asked him about *how* the bloody smear marks got there. But Burke remembered how they got there. He remembered it well. He was, after all, the one who put them there. It was his blood, which ran straight from his fingertips as they lightly stroked the circle of the sun the morning he obtained the flag. His hand bled underneath his shame for a long time that morning; it was a detail of the war Burke never forgot. His bloody hand that morning looked much like it did the morning he first landed in Japan.

Burke's hand was covered in blood. There was glass everywhere. In his lap, shards of windshield glistened against the sun; drops of blood had formed around the shards and caused the reflection of the sun against them to turn a dazzling red. In the air was an intense smell of burning metal and engine fumes, which wafted fiercely into his nose, causing him to stir awake. He unbuckled his seatbelt and tried to lift himself up from his seat. A hot, searing pain torched his back, going all the way down his bottom and thighs. He tried once again to lift himself, fighting past the tugging pain that was attempting to drag him back into the seat. Staggering clumsily as he stood up in his cockpit, Lieutenant Burke examined his surroundings. The world had gone fuzzy, and the light that poked through the trees seemed brighter than usual.

Behind him, fallen trees and flattened bushes marked his descent pattern. Burke's head was throbbing harder than it ever had in his life. There was no blood coming from anywhere on his head, minus a gash on his upper forehead, which gave him hope that he was doing okay. He later figured he had sustained a concussion from the blow to his head, which explained his dizziness. His stomach churned over once, madly causing him to double over and vomit down the side of his plane. As he bent across the plane, his knee shot a pain upwards through his body and he buckled.

Somewhere towards the front of his plane, Leo's bird had gone down. There was no telling how Leo had turned out but Burke knew that he needed to get to Leo fast if there was going to be any hope at all. After several attempts, Burke managed to pull himself out of the cockpit and slide down the side of the plane to the ground below. As soon as his feet touched the ground, his legs gave way to excruciating pain and he buckled once again. Slowly, Burke began to drag himself forward to a fallen tree and used it to pull himself up. Inside, he panicked while a hundred scenarios raced through his mind.

What am I doing here? he thought to himself. *How did I… why?* His thoughts were so sporadic it scared him even more. As he dragged himself along the tree, Burke tried hard to draw enough oxygen into his lungs to make a break towards Leo. It was almost impossible. He could hardly breathe. His chest felt as though there was a devil trying to squeeze the oxygen back out with his fiery bare hands. There was nothing in the world he wanted to do more than to sit on the tree trunk for a while longer and shut his eyes for a moment. Then, the thought of Leo, sitting alone in his cockpit, spurred him to action.

Burke edged along the side of the tree as long as he could. The smooth surface of the bark was stained with a streak of crimson from his hand. The ground beneath his feet was shifting and tumbling all about, making it hard to even look down. Somehow, he was able to forge ahead by stumbling from tree to tree, hanging onto them for support. Every other step was infinitely harder than the last. The pain in his knee and in his head took turns throbbing so that each step carried him a shorter distance than the step before.

Monkeys cackled wildly in the trees overhead, dashing across from branch to branch. They made him surge with angry energy. Burke even reached down and gripped the handle of his .45 sidearm, entertaining the idea of shooting each of them out of the trees, one by one. Burke convinced himself not to pull his sidearm and start shooting. He only had twelve bullets and none to spare. He wasn't a good enough aim to really hit any of them in the first place. Then, the thought crossed his mind that he would at least need to save two of those bullets, in case things with Leo were worse than he hoped. It was an escape plan, as good as any he had. John caressed his holster, feeling the weight of the firearm as if checking to make sure it was still there. The handle of the 1911 was cool to the touch and sent chills straight into his soul.

Eventually, after having limped his way past enough trees, Burke reached the clearing. His legs burned as if he had just run his first marathon. It was still hard to breathe and the oxygen still put up a fight on its way into his lungs. Leo's plane was now visible, nearly thirty yards in front of Burke. The damage to the outside of the plane wasn't as bad as Burke had initially envisioned. One wing was broken in half and the other had shredded across the ground on impact. Debris and metal were scattered everywhere along the ground hundreds of feet in every direction. Somehow, the image of Leo's downed plane actually instilled an energy inside him. The cockpit was turned away, making it hard to see anything, but Burke thought he could still see the outline of Leo's head through the smoky glass.

Burke bolted towards the plane as fast as he could. "Leo!" he shouted. "Leo! I'm coming!"

There was no reply or sign of movement from inside the cockpit. The closer Burke got, the harder he ran. By the time he reached the cockpit, Burke had been in nearly an-all out sprint, or at least as good a sprint as he could manage. He used the debris and rocks to claw his way up to the cockpit. Pushing broken glass and metal out of the way, Burke finally managed to see inside.

It was bad. Leo was a bloody mess. His left arm was mangled and chewed up and, from what Burke could tell, Leo's left shoulder had taken a hard hit as well. In fact, all of Leo's left half had taken the brunt of the impact. His left hand looked almost like jell-o, dangling limp and loose from his wrist. With his right arm, Leo clutched his waistline. Blood covered his legs, waist, and seat.

"Leo, look at me buddy," Burke begged. He shoved more glass and debris out of his way. "Leo, I need you to look at me. Please look me in the eye! Please!"

Slowly, Leo's body began to shift and his head rose only slightly. Shards of glass had done a number on Leo's cheeks and jaw line. His whole face was covered with little cut marks and lacerations. Leo's eyes, somehow, had managed to maintain a glint of hope and his face gave way to a light, ironic smile. It was the first of a few good signs. "Howdy, John," he wheezed.

"Hiya, Leo."

"Helluva landin'. Think they noticed us comin' in?" he asked.

John smiled. "Maybe."

Leo tried moving on his own. He didn't get very far. His side was in very bad shape and his right arm had moved out far enough for Burke to better assess the damage. "Do I look as bad as I feel?" asked Leo.

Burke twinged, fearful of telling the truth. If he told him the truth, Leo would have gotten hysterical which would have made it even harder to move him from the crash site, which they needed to do fast. Burke shook his head as lightly as he could. "You look about as good as I did after those leeches," John replied.

"Ah, hell, John. That bad?" Leo joked. It sounded halfway serious, though.

Leo was in no shape to move on his own, so Burke bent across the cockpit and unbuckled his seatbelt for him. Leo shifted himself so Burke could grab his under his armpits and pull him out of the cockpit. The two had to stop halfway through and take a break, but eventually they managed to help Leo out and slide down to the ground without enduring too much more pain. They crawled over to a nearby stump and sat back down, Leo sitting sideways so that his wounds faced up and out. Once on the ground and in the light, Burke could tell that the gash along Leo's waist was even worse than it appeared in the plane. Quickly, Burke pulled off his jacket and placed it hard over Leo's wound to help stop the blood. "Press hard," he instructed Leo, switching hands and letting Leo apply his own pressure.

"It hurts a lot, John," Leo whispered shakily.

"I know, buddy, you just need to keep pushing hard on it."
Burke looked around the area for anything useful. Suddenly, the sight
of Leo's cockpit reminded him of the radios. There was a chance the
radios still worked and they would be able to send a signal back to
base. It was a slight chance, but it brought a glimmer of hope. "Is
your radio still working?" he asked Leo excitedly.

"I dunno; I didn't think to try," Leo replied.

Immediately, Burked hobbled over to the plane and climbed
back up to the cockpit, grabbing Leo's radio equipment. He spun the
dials in every direction and tried every signal he knew: "Plane down.
Need help. Mayday."

Nothing.

The radio still had power coming through to it, but none of
the signals yielded any response; assumedly, none were going out
either. Burke slunk over the side of the plane, defeated. He thought
of the radio in his own cockpit, which he had failed to try before
leaving. By that point, Burke's plane was too far away for Leo to walk
to and it would have been incredibly risky, if not insane, for them to
go back. The Japanese were no doubt halfway to the other crash site
by then. Even if the equipment worked and they were able to get a
signal out, it would have been for nothing if the Japanese picked
them up first. Sitting in Leo's cockpit was the moment Burke lost
what remained of his hope.

If Leo had not fallen from the sky with him, John would have
burst into tears. For some reason, Leo's scared timid gaze made
Burke suck back his own fear in hopes of squelching Leo's fear. Leo

was afraid because he didn't know what was going to happen next, and he looked at John as if *he* did. John sat there, thinking at a hundred miles an hour and getting nowhere. Without hope, there wasn't much left for Burke to pull ideas from.

The best idea John had was to get out of the area. The longer they sat there, the longer they became sitting ducks waiting to be cooked. Burke slid back down off of the plane's nose and limped over to Leo. With his good shoulder, he dipped underneath Leo's right arm and helped him to his feet. "Keep pushing hard on that," he told Leo, pointing to Leo's wound.

"Where are we goin'?" Leo asked. John didn't know. He certainly didn't want Leo to know that, though. Unable to think of anything to say, Burke said nothing.

"What's the plan?" Leo begged him further.

John walked Leo out of the clearing towards the south as he wondered how to respond. "We are getting out of here first," he told him.

"But where are we gonna go?"

"To the south."

"Is ther' help that way? Can we get off th' island from there?" Leo continued.

The truth was, Burke had no real good reason to pick the south. He figured that the soldiers who shot them down to begin with were back in the north and the men had turned their planes away from the ground fire to the east, so anywhere but north or east seemed like a good way to go. Leo kept begging John for an answer, his fear welling up in tears around his bloodshot eyes.

"Yes, Leo, it's a safe way to go," Burke eventually responded. Deep down, he felt he had delivered the biggest lie of his entire life.

"Are we gonna make it out, John? Everthin's gonna be okay, right?" Leo asked.

"You bet, buddy," said Burke, digging deeper. Suddenly, Leo winced and cried out in horrible pain, slowing them down. Behind them, the cackle of monkeys rose shrilly over the treetops in response to Leo's cry of pain.

"Are you okay?" Burke asked, concerned.

"My side is killin' me," Leo admitted.

"I'll patch you up, Leo; we just got to get out of the clearing, alright?" Burke felt disgusted with himself. He had honestly no idea what to do with Leo next and was doubtful he would be able to get much further out of the clearing. Burke just wanted out – to get far, far away from the clearing and wreckage as possible. He almost wished he were home. But, he could not tell this to Leo; it would have killed him on the spot to realize the truth: they weren't going home.

"We're gonna git outa here, right John?" Leo asked. Burke said nothing at first. "Right, John?" he cried.

John shook his head. "Yeah, we're going to—"

He stopped.

"What is it?" Leo pleaded with him.

"Shh."

"John, what is it?" Leo said even louder.

"Shh!"

It was there, in the distance, to the northeast, that John heard motors rumbling low and fast through the trees. They were searching. "We got to go," John told Leo quickly, taking him back under his arm. "Come on!"

TWO

It was loud, nearly deafening. From above and all around, there were sounds of rustling, moving, creeping, and groaning creatures emerging from behind nearly every tree, leaf, and plant. Burke laid alongside a sleeping Leo, underneath the shelter of a mossy outset. Burke was wide-eyed and alert.

A crack of a tree limb. The rustling of some leaves. The barking of a wild animal somewhere off in the distance. It was hard to tell what was approaching – or not approaching – through the thick darkness that had settled on the rainforest after the sun set. For hours, the men laid there out of sight as the night brought with it a bevy of unsettled creatures moving about in the shadows.

The two had managed to sneak out of the clearing and take refuge nearly a kilometer away from the wreckage. Burke had wanted to be further away, but for all intents and purposes he was surprised they had even made it that far. When they came upon a discreet place to rest, they immediately settled down and took shelter for the night, hoping to gain back their energy; for what, Burke was not yet sure.

The two curled up close to each other for warmth as the bitter cold swept in with the night, and together, they whispered prayers for mercy, doubtful that mercy would come. Leo was growing weaker and weaker, growing paler by the hour. His body was shivering and twitching madly in pain next to Burke. Things were growing worse.

It had taken the men all day to get to where they were. Earlier in the afternoon, the patrols that had assisted in shooting them out of the sky had done a clumsy sweep of the area looking for them. Leo and Burke had managed to stay low and quiet, out of sight and hidden, for most of the day. By evening time, the patrols had long since given up their search and decided to simply let the men succumb to the elements. The patrols knew, as did Burke and Leo deep down, that if the explosions didn't bring them to that fate, the elements would. By nightfall, Burke and Leo's goal had become to try and gain back a semblance of energy, but more so, to survive through the night. The noise of the rainforest assured them that it was going to be a long night.

Leo rustled awake, hardly coherent, and began to make a fuss.

"Shh, go back to sleep," Burke whispered in his ear, keeping one eye on the alert and the other on Leo.

"W-what... d-don't... Christmas everybody..." Leo struggled to keep himself together.

"That's right, it's almost Christmas," Burke replied. "Go back to bed."

Leo slouched his head back to the ground. Burke noticed a cold sweat had broken out all along Leo's neck and down his back.

Suddenly, off in the distance, a group of plants flung about in a commotion. The commotion shifted quickly from the plants on the ground to the trees above and darted overhead. John pulled Leo in closer, his heart beating so loudly that he could hear it in his head. Creatures hummed and buzzed from leaves and ditches as if in response to the commotion. Burke eventually settled himself underneath the outset and slowed the pace of his fearfully darting eyes. Then he huffed, almost into a smile, at the irony. That night reminded him of working at the zoo back in Illinois. Thinking about that damned zoo was actually, for the first time, a good thing for him. For some odd but gracious reason, the first memory that came to mind about the zoo was the only *good* memory Burke had ever had of the place.

It was 1941. John had been working at the zoo for less than a month. His uncle, who was no better at handling himself under alcohol than McDuff or John's mother, had gotten him the job. They needed money, so the choice not to work was never available. Burke's mother had had a hard time keeping the two of them going on what little housework she picked up whenever she could. Cleaning houses for snobby do-gooders did not pay much, especially at that time, and when most every penny went to assisting her "habit," things got even harder. John's uncle had supported the two of them as best he could, but he had problems of his own. Money and jobs were scarce. When the zoo started hiring young men to clean up the grounds, people flocked out of the woodwork to get the position. John's uncle was good friends with the owner – as birds of a feather tended to flock. Before long, and after a few good beers, John's uncle had talked his nephew into a job cleaning up animal pens.

Funny as it was, cleaning up animal crap actually paid Burke more than cleaning up human crap paid his mother. It was anything but glamorous, but it put food on the table. Years later, when Burke's own kids were grown up, one of his daughters told him that she wanted to start a business cleaning up dog crap for people who were too lazy to do it themselves. Burke's wife, of course, had a brain hemorrhage when she heard about her daughter's plan. Burke actually liked the idea. He knew that his daughter realized an essential principle of life that he himself learned at the zoo – poop pays. While working for the zoo, Burke never did earn much of a wage, but neither did his mother (or anybody for that matter). At least when he combined his salary with her's, they had one full paycheck.

McDuff had owned the zoo for a while. He started working at the zoo in the twenties – when things were good – after buying it from a relative with money that he managed to sneak back into the States after the War. In the worst of the thirties, McDuff had managed to keep the place open by selling goat milk and composting manure for farmers at a low, low price. The zoo had gone from a zoo to a dump pretty fast. All of the animals had to be sold, minus the ones that proved useful – goats, sheep, so on. It had essentially become a glorified urban farm that smelled like a pair of old gym shoes. McDuff also turned into a dump during this time, too. He had taken up drinking like it had become an Olympic sport. Before long, he started smelling worse than the animals. He even stopped cleaning the pens like he used to and, by that point, had fired everybody who had worked there before. It had gotten to the point where even the animals had a hard time going near him. Whether that was because McDuff smelled so bad or drank so much, nobody could be for certain. By the time Burke got a job working for McDuff, there was essentially nothing McDuff *could* do at the zoo anymore on account of his drinking. McDuff's job became "supervising" the men as they performed all the duties he couldn't, due to his inevitable intoxication. The workers quickly learned that the secret to a good day at the zoo was to not cross paths, or even see McDuff at any point in the day. This, however, proved easier said than done.

However, even between the drinking and the prostitutes McDuff often hired for unreasonable prices, he managed to raise enough money to purchase a camel. All of the workers, especially John, wondered where and why he bought the camel. None of them ever got an explanation. One day, during their regular working hours, McDuff paraded the camel into the zoo and informed the men that the creature was going to be added to their responsibilities – without any extra pay. Burke thought to himself that his boss probably had plans to milk it or sell whatever came out of it to the people of Illinois, which was exactly McDuff's drunken thinking when he bought the animal. This is what made McDuff a first-rate idiot.

Once the camel arrived, though, life around the zoo began to take a turn. At random, the men working each day would be approached and asked to drop whatever they were doing to go pay homage to the camel. This puzzled the men, who were generally pissed off that they had to interact with the boss on any level in the first place. Worse, every morning one of the boys was tasked with the duty of taking the poor, embarrassed creature outside the zoo walls for a walk. Both the animal and the boy doing this awful thing were equally humiliated by this ridiculous request. McDuff believed, however, that this parade would drum up interest for the zoo. It didn't. No one cared. No one even noticed. The other pens just got dirtier.

Eventually, the kid who was tasked with this inane job had had enough. His name was Olin and he was not but a couple of years younger than Burke. Burke liked him, mostly because Olin hated the camel with a hatred that the rest of the workers only wished they had the guts to possess; the camel, in turn, hated McDuff for this outrageous prejudice, and McDuff in turn hated all of them. Every day, Olin took the poor, dumb creature out for an hour, stood on the sidewalk outside the zoo like an idiot, and watched as people ignored him. The camel usually just stood there too, smacking his lips with such indifferent apathy that it rivaled only Olin's own apathy. Olin only wanted to do his job, his actual job, which involved doing something productive but was forced to stand out in the cold every day with the camel. Finally one morning, Olin decided that he and the camel had had enough. He promptly walked the camel back inside the zoo in protest, which caused McDuff to come scurrying out of his office in a drunken stupor and beat the poor kid half to death. It was so bad, McDuff even slapped Burke once across the face just for watching.

114

After McDuff had had his fun and had sauntered back into his office, Olin, in an act of defiance Burke had never before seen, marched the camel outside the zoo, made a bee-line with it to McDuff's junky Ford, and waited there until the creature defecated all around his car. Olin, of course, helped the creature get its "point" across all over the hood and windshield. By the time McDuff had notice and stormed out of his office, both Olin and the camel were long gone and their "point" had become frozen solid all over McDuff's car.

Burke never saw the camel or Olin again. And as he sat there, defenseless and cold on the jungle floor in Japan, all Burke could think about was Olin and that camel. He grinned to himself, a grin genuine and real. He had always held a deep respect for Olin. The kid could have taken off, Burke often thought; all of the men who worked at that zoo wanted to take off and never come back. Olin, however, actually had the balls to do it *and* to save the one animal at that zoo that still had a shred of dignity left. Burke had always respected that. While sitting on the dank and cold jungle floor of Japan, there was nothing in the world that Burke wanted to do more than to take off. The only problem was, there was nowhere to take off to.

At his side, Burke could feel Leo's frail body push up against him gently in shallow breaths. He felt bad for the kid. He wanted Leo to at least have his dignity, if anything. *Hell, I want to at least die with dignity too!* he thought. There was no way they were going to get out of there. Not even the Jarheads could make it to Japan on foot – they were hardly even halfway there. The Navy certainly wasn't covering any ground past Buka and New Ireland for a while. The only men who had access to the main island were flyboys and the only thing they were carrying were bombs with no room for passengers. Burke and Leo had become trapped, like animals, with no way of leaving. Not even an act of defiance would allow them their freedom.

It was then that Burke felt his sidearm weigh heavy on his mind. It was something. A choice. A way out. Burke knew well what they did to prisoners of war; he had heard more than enough stories. Burke thought of the poor Japanese pilot who had landed in the water just weeks before, outside the base in Guadalcanal. For that pilot, it came down to dying in the dark void below or being sent to die on land under the dark void of the sky. He at least had the luxury of choosing what he wanted, picking what he thought was best. Burke knew that he wasn't going to be able to run far, to escape his fate, but he knew that he at least had the opportunity to choose.

He sauntered away from Leo a safe distance and crawled onto his knees. From his holster, he carefully slid out his sidearm. Its nickel-plating reflected a menacing ray of moonlight back at him. As he turned it from side to side, getting used to its presence, he could make out the light engraving that ornamented the barrel: "*Colt .45 1911.*" Burke turned the weapon around to face him, innocently at first, his finger off the trigger. The barrel was much longer than he had imagined it would be. Inside the barrel, an evil lurked amidst the cloudy blackness, waiting to bite on command. Burke turned the gun back around and took the heft of the weapon in his hands. His fingers caressed the side of the trigger. It was an option.

"What wouldya think Parker'd say?" Leo whispered.

Burke whipped around to Leo, startled. Leo's sad eyes gazed up from where he lay on the muddy ground. Burke shook his head in fear and confusion.

"What wouldya think Parker'd say?" Leo repeated, pleading desperately. Tears began to well up in his eyes and he sat up on his elbow as best he could. "He'd say there's a better way than crawlin' inside that thing there and dyin', John."

Burke continued to shake his head and turned the gun around to look inside the black abyss of the barrel.

"Come on, John. You knew Parker," Leo continued, now begging sincerely. "He was all abut' God's graces above. Don't do it, John. Don't rob God of his graces, huh? P-please… d-don't leave me here like 'dis. I-I'm scared, John, I'm real scared…"

Slowly, John lowered his weapon. Streams began to fall from his eyes and travel wildly down his cheeks. "You believe in that crap? You believe in God's graces?" he asked Leo, gazing sullenly into the middle distance.

Leo nodded emphatically. "I ain't *not* seen his graces yet," he said.

John moved his weapon back into his holster, the weight of the weapon sinking deeply on his side.

"Don't do it, John," Leo added. "Don't take God's graces from him."

I'm just trying to make his graces happen faster, John thought to himself. *It's about damn time it happened.*

Deep down, Burke felt neither grace nor mercy anywhere. They were lost, cold, hungry, bleeding, and dying in a land filled with people who would relish their slow and painful death. There was no mercy to be found, no grace. If God wasn't going to move into action, John stood ready and waiting to move for him.

"You gotta promise me now, John," Leo cried. "Don't do it. Don't go like that."

Burke winced. This was the last thing he wanted to hear, and was not the kind of promise he was going to be able to keep. "Leo, I—"

"Promise a dyin' man that, John. P-please..."

Burke bit down, grinding his teeth. The words did not come readily, but he eventually whispered, "I promise."

Leo let off and laid back down, whispering a prayer of thanks as he dozed back off. Burke remained on his knees a while longer, the weight of his gun still pulling him to the ground. Eventually, he lifted himself up, moved back underneath the shelter of the outset and closed his eyes as the sounds of the jungle shrieked madly about him. The thought of his weapon never left his mind. And, as it was, it would not be the last time Burke unholstered his gun either.

THREE

The raindrops bounced off of Leo's chest in every direction with each blow of Burke's punches. He had been punching Leo's chest in the chilling drizzle for nearly twenty minutes in unparalleled desperation. As the rain poured down his long, sturdy chin and onto Leo's cold body, the last shred of hope disappeared from Burke's heart.

Surely God is not this cruel, he thought.

Abandoned and alone, he sat in the wet jungle thick, tears bursting forth with every sob. Leo's bloody corpse hung limp in Burke's arms. He was gone.

"DAMMIT!" Burke shot out towards the sky. The fire and pain in his voice bellowed out like smoke from his mouth. God did not respond. "What are you doing!? What are you thinking!? Is this what you wanted!? SCREW YOU, screw it all!" he screamed. "I HATE YOU... I-I hate..."

He sobbed, feeling deep down that all the world had stood still. Burke had never wept that hard in all his life. Blood was everywhere, most of it from Leo. Burke examined the mess and remembered a story from the Bible he had heard when he was a child. In church, on an Easter service his mother dragged him to before going to the bar, they had told him that before his execution, Jesus wept so hard that blood ran down from his pores. Before the war, Burke figured it was nothing more than an over-glorified line of crap. But while he sat in the midst of the enemy, he knew without a doubt, that it was certainly possible. As he wept, feeling lonely and abandoned, the very blood in his veins felt as though it had turned to gasoline and lit on fire. The burning made its way through his body, into his eyes, and streamed down his cheeks. The feeling came over him like a tidal wave. It was the most alone Burke had felt in his entire life.

There was but a bud of anger inside him, just enough to sear Burke down to his core. Releasing it, he pounded the ground furiously and cursed some more: "Screw... you... dammit... oh, God..." The words came in and out of beats in between sobs. While each man must die alone, Burke was left to *face* death by himself. And there he sat, alone, waiting for death.

Burke spent a good deal of that morning simply looking at Leo's peaceful face. He was only a kid, just a few years younger than Burke. Leo was thousands of miles away from family and thousands of miles away from anybody he really knew. Chances were, he would never even make it back to them. His body would remain far away in the jungle of Japan. In a week or two, Burke imagined, Leo's family would receive a letter from a plainly dressed officer who had rung their doorbell. They wouldn't even have to open the letter to know that it said Leo had been taken by the skies and there was no hope of bringing him back. There would be an apology on behalf of the U.S. government, and condolences offered for a man they never knew. They would provide Leo's family with an empty casket and a flag, in due time. The only person who would ever get to really see or bury Leo was John. His face was the last thing Leo saw and Burke would be the last one to see Leo's. As he looked upon Leo's face one last time, Burke noticed his eyelids, closed gently over his eyes, and his mouth, which remained peacefully closed. Through his uniform, Leo's body grew colder and colder and his skin became a light grey.

Burke stood up and searched the area while he wiped away his tears, looking for a place to bury Leo. Finding nowhere suitable, Burke eventually gathered together a small rock to place behind Leo's head and a few flowers. He worked carefully to move Leo's arms to lay across his diaphragm. The noise of the jungle never subsided as he worked, not even of out respect.

As he finished positioning Leo's body, the sun began to poke through from the east and gleamed off of the drizzle still falling softly from the skies. Leo's body laid there, surrounded by green moss and thick grass, with his face just barely catching the warmth of the sun. It was just enough to bring out what color was left in his skin; it was just enough to remind Burke one last time what Leo had looked like while alive. Burke smiled. He was a good kid, John thought, saved by mercy from the hell of another fate. Reverently, John said his goodbyes and bid Leo farewell.

Staggering away from Leo's body, Burke eventually collapsed onto his knees. The tears in his eyes still fogged his field of vision and the blood inside his veins still burned in agony. *What am I doing out here*, he wondered again. *I'm not even 30; I'm a boy. A child. What am I doing here?* His thoughts raced, unrelenting. He was a *child* living a life that few *men* should ever have to live.

It was then that John felt his hip grow heavy. At his waist, the nickel-plated sidearm tugged alluringly for his attention. Suddenly, he remembered his options. Somewhere, out in the jungle, was a patrol group, still looking for whoever had survived the crash. On Burke's hip was a pistol that invited him to do what the Japanese were probably going to do to him anyway. He was the pilot who was given a chance to decide his own demise.

Slowly, he pulled his sidearm out of its holster. It felt even heavier in his hands than it did the night before, as if the raindrops falling on it added their weight to its bulk. The mechanisms inside the weapon jostled as his hand quaked and trembled. Letting out a heave, and feeling his heart sink, he let out a small, faint whisper:

"I'm sorry... I didn't mean what I said... I don't hate, you. Sorr..."

His mind brought forth all the things that he had left unaccounted for, loose ends he would never be able to tie up. His mother was still alive, as best he knew – he prayed she would make it without him. Burke even forgave McDuff for being McDuff. He didn't know if it was truly in his heart to forgive him, but he thought it would add up to a few good points during his judgment if he did.

Finally, John prayed for his soul. In his heart, he doubted if God would ever forgive him for what he was about to do, but he figured he'd take his chances and hope for the best.

Burke decided to do it as fast as he could. It seemed best. He positioned himself against the side of a large boulder and gazed off, down the sloping hillside in front of him. He braced himself against the boulder, pushing hard with his legs as if to wedge himself into the rock and not move. He closed his eyes and said one last prayer for luck, or grace. He opened his eyes. Salty tears scorched his eyelids and ran down his face. Quickly, he shoved the front of the gun in his mouth as fast as he could, his hands trembling madly. The pad of his fingertip snaked around the trigger and caressed it lightly. A second went by. Two seconds. Three.

"What wouldya think Parker'd say?" came a voice loudly from behind.

Burke stopped, turning around and looking behind him. It wasn't a thought; it was a voice; he knew it. He leaned over and saw Leo's body, still lying lifeless on the ground. He shook his head in disbelief.

"You promised."

He shook his head in disbelief, looking around madly. Carefully, he lowered his weapon and sat back against the rock, taking in a quivering breath and letting it out slowly. His heart pounded against the wall of his chest and the blood rushed back into the limbs of his body.

"I'm sorry," he whispered.

From all around, the noise of the jungle made its way back to his cognizance. Holstering his weapon, Burke leaned his head back against the rock, staring off into the sky from which he had fallen. Through cracks in the dark, grey clouds was a streak of bright blue that came down upon him as quiet and gentle as a ray of sun. It was as if the god of the void was up there, behind the clouds and beyond the crack in the sky, still aware.

"Whatever it is, show it to me," John told him.

The sky said nothing.

"Where is it? Parker said you'd give it, but…"

The sky replied with nothing.

Nodding his head, Burke stood, using the rock as a way to climb up. From his holster, the gun, which hadn't been put in all the way, slipped back out and fell onto the ground. Annoyed, Burke bent down to pick it up. On the ground, fallen next to it, was the small leather Bible from his jumpsuit pocket. The leather cover of the book was tattered and some of the pages had collected blood. At some point, the little book had fallen out of Burke's pocket. Swiftly, he swiped it back up, along with his gun, and put it back where it belonged. He gazed back up at the crack in the sky. From beyond, the blue sky shied away, still smiling at him, as the grey clouds covered it back up.

Burke left, leaving Leo's body alone in the jungle. As he walked away, Burke turned to Leo, checking on his body. His body lay there, peaceful and untouched. It pained Burke to leave. It had hurt to be left. It was a hurt he never wanted to feel again.

Many years later, the hurt returned. She had been in the hospital for little over a week; he hadn't slept in days. Even in that bed, with every tube imaginable stuck in every nook and cranny of her body, she was just as beautiful as ever to him. He had never been much of an affectionate man, somewhat regrettably. In his entire life with her, John's children had seen him kiss his wife less than a handful of times. But on the night she died, he sat near her bedside and cradled her head gently, letting her white curly hair make its way through his fingers. That was the last time he kissed her on the lips. Hours later, she finally passed. And as he let go of her, the pain of being left was infinitely harder than when he left Leo alone in the jungle. His dearest love was gone, and he was alone.

The nurses entered her room and, touching him on the shoulder, gently asked him to go into the hallway. He didn't hear them, not just because his hearing was mostly gone, but because he didn't want to. She was still as beautiful as ever; he didn't want to leave. As they helped his frail, graying body to his feet, the image of his lovely wife was all he saw. In the hallway, his children took him into their arms and ushered him out of the hospital. Even though they took him home, he never really left her room.

That night, John's eldest son stayed with him, insistent that he not be by himself. Somehow, his son knew that the thing John feared the most was being alone. And while the rest of his family went to their beds to sleep, the morning hours approaching quickly, John stayed in the living room, sitting in her chair quietly, somber.

They buried her in November. The afternoon turned out to be quiet and cool. It was open casket. When they arrived at the funeral home, John was the first to go in, ushered in by his son who followed nearly ten paces behind. John's wife lay in the same peace in which he had left her, dressed in the yellow and black dress John's daughters had picked out especially for her. He always liked that dress, more than anything. Her arms were up by her diaphragm and she held a small bouquet of white flowers that her children knew she would want. It was simple. John especially liked that.

He and his family buried her with dignity and grace. When the funeral was over, John went back home, requesting to be alone, and returned to her chair in their living room. The house was quiet, vacant. And there in the quiet, tucked away from the others, he cried gently and made his peace with God. From the dining room, the flag watched him, but not in any sinister way; it watched him with a somber eye, as if it too were grieving. There, the two stared, man and flag, remembering how it felt to be alone. They both knew the feeling.

The morning following his wife's burial, Burke immediately made arrangements to be cremated and buried with her. This came as a shock to his children and was met with much resistance. This of course fell on his deaf ears. As they began to argue with him, Burke simply raised his hand and bowed his head: "Let it be. Please. For me." And that was all there was to the discussion.

In May of the following year, John Oscar Burke gave up his final breaths. During his last day on earth, the only thoughts he had were towards his wife. Nothing excited him more than the thought of going to be with her again, and that was exactly what he did. And so he was buried, alongside his beautiful wife, who was dressed to the nines, and neither of them had to be alone ever again.

FOUR

The road on all sides was dense, covered by thick leaves, branches, and shrubs. Overhead, the sun remained mostly hidden behind the enormous canopy of trees. The small size of the country of Japan was lost on Burke as he carefully gauged where to go next. He eventually aimed his bearings toward the south, knowing that in enough time, he could hit the Pacific coast. Then it would just be a matter of getting over the water and back home, a small hurdle he would figure out later. The air was frigid, worse than any cold Burke had ever experienced before. Somehow the air had grown dank and heavy, making it hard to breath. Shivering, he covered himself as best he could underneath the thin lining of his jumpsuit; he had relinquished his jacket to Leo and even if he had taken it up when he left, the blood-soaked cloth would not have offered him much warmth.

Burke managed to hobble about half a mile to the south before he ran into a stream. Gazing downstream, he figured his best bet was to follow it, hoping that whatever it led to provided either warmth, food, or a swift end to the bitter cold of the winter day.

Hours droned by without any reprieve. Burke's leg began to throb angrily and his neck was started to become stiff and aggravated as he passed the six mile mark. Several times, Burke stopped to gain a semblance of energy again before charging on. By the late afternoon, he was tired, hungry, sore, grumpy, and sick of the jungle.

By around 1700 hours that afternoon, Burke had begun running out of steam. He had begun praying for some sort of salvation, a beacon of hope; unfortunately, something quite hopeless lay waiting for him at the end of the stream.

As he was sitting down, taking a rest break, a sauntering collection of footsteps broke through the brush. Ducking down out of sight, Burke made out the tan color of standard issue Japanese military pants poking through the twigs and shrubs. Ahead of him, thirty yards at most, was a Japanese platoon man. He carried with him nothing more than a rifle and a backpack. As he walked, the soldier's helmet bobbed goofily up and down, in sync with the his high-pitched whistles. With each whistle, the soldier would wait a moment before whistling again, waiting for the birds above him to report back. He continued conversing with the birds, their conversation growing infinitely more serious. Abruptly, the soldier stopped, just fifteen yards shy of Burke's position.

Burke ducked behind a log and hugged the ground, praying he was out of sight. Neither man moved a muscle. Chances were, there were plenty of other soldiers not far off from the stream, men that Burke had no intention of being introduced to. Suddenly, there was a sound. More whistling, different this time, as if the soldier was whistling to draw attention to something. Then another sound. A zipper. Then another. Urinating. Then another. A whistle signifying relief.

It took what muscles weren't working to keep Burke hidden to help him avoid smiling, given the circumstances. In his mind, he remembered all of the briefings he got about the Japanese from his superiors – fierce warriors who had little pity on their enemy. When he was in training, Burke imagined a people unruly, unkempt, and dirty from all of the war-torn battles they faced as they carried with them bullet-scarred flags which flew proudly from their platoons. And there he was, listening to some poor sap take a piss. The Great Escape, this was not.

After the soldier had made his contribution to Mother Earth, he performed a jiggle-dance and turned back from whence he came, on his merry little way. Burke fell in step, keeping usually twenty yards or so between him and the soldier. Eventually, he was led to a small clearing in the jungle. Tents and supplies were set up everywhere, as were soldiers. A large, courageous Japanese flag flew proudly over their heads, keeping watch in the sky. The soldier that led Burke to this place greeted a group of friends with a sly remark, pointing to something off in the distance. The others shot back a host of commentary followed by laughter. The peeing soldier did not appreciate their opinion and promptly flipped the other men off. It was nice to know, Burke thought, that the fierce enemy the Jarheads warned them about at least had a sense of humor not unlike their own. Burke even swore that he spotted one of the soldiers making fun of the Navy; one of the soldiers made a pathetic whimpering noise to a group of listeners while he pantomimed a puny tugboat. The others let out a wild burst of laughter, slapping each other in a sense of enlightened camaraderie. Burke shook his head and smiled; nobody seemed to respect the Navy – not even the people the Navy boys said were most afraid of them. It would have made Burke feel somewhat sorry for them too, if it he didn't find it so funny.

Burke was able to count twelve or so men in the camp. They seemed to have set up a sort of temporary, make-shift camp along Burke's route to "somewhere." Most of the tents were filled with nothing more than supply crates and other assorted goods; these soldiers were most likely on an errand to deliver supplies to other encampments. Burke sat there for nearly three hours, watching them interact and putz around, shooting the breeze with one another. By evening, the men were joined by two other soldiers who had come in from the south, most likely from patrolling the area. The others questioned them and listened passively to their report, which did not seem to shake any of their ground.

From his perch, Burke carefully watched the Japanese soldiers do an assortment of things, much of which involved them drinking, burping, and joking around. It struck him as being much like life was for him at Guadalcanal, only on the other side of the lines. Mostly, though, Burke kept his eyes on the crates filled to the brim with MREs. Burke's stomach roared ferociously as he watched the men throw the MREs back and forth in hungry excitement; he was surprised the soldiers didn't hear the rumbling of his stomach for themselves.

Burke made up his mind to wait until some of the men had gone to bed before sneaking down to get into their food. This took a while, as most of the men spent a great deal of time joking and drinking, which only gave Burke more time to formulate a plan of action and execute it in his head a few million times. He spotted a tent where most of the soldiers exited from carrying food; he decided he would make his way to the rear of it, swipe whatever supplies he could, and make his way out the same way he came in.

Eventually, his opportunity came. There were only two men still awake and roaming, keeping watch as patrol. One of them moseyed his way carelessly around the camp while the other sat close to the fire lazily. Burke edged his way towards the camp, cutting out wide in the jungle and coming up near his mark slowly and quietly. Carefully, he approached the rear entrance of the tent. Inside, Burke could see one of the men sleeping soundly on his cot. Across from him was another Japanese soldier, taking out a cigarette and scrounging around his things for a lighter. Finally, the soldier got hacked off, unable to find it, and shoved a nearby supply bag to the ground in frustration. He then spotted his sleeping friend's lighter lying at the foot of the man's bed. The soldier swiped up the lighter, jeering in whispers at his sleeping cohort, and dodged out the front of the tent to light up. This was Burke's cue.

Darting into the tent, Burke searched everywhere all at once. The first thing he grabbed, and was glad he did, was a coat from the front of a vacant bed. The Japanese uniform jacket fit snug around his tall frame but had enough heft to keep him reasonably insulated. Next, Burke began hunting for food. The spicy odor of tobacco in the tent overwhelmed his senses at first, making it hard to smell anything else. Soon, though, he found what he was looking for – a pile of MRE's stacked at the back corner of the tent. He figured he must have missed them on his way in. Falling onto his knees, he lunged into them – as quietly as he could manage – and, out of his sheer hunger, tore into one immediately. Wildly, he began shoveling uncooked, packaged muck into his throat as fast as he could. He smiled. The taste of food was almost more excitement than he could manage. As he shoveled food in quickly, he looked down at the slick, brown MRE package, which was covered in Japanese writing. Only three words were distinguishable, primarily because they were written in English in tiny, gold print: "Made in America." It took him by surprise. *What on earth is...*

Suddenly, he heard someone rustling behind him. Then he heard moaning. It was coming from the sleeping man. He was coming awake.

"He-!?" the man started, noticing Burke.

Without a thought, Burke whipped out his sidearm from its holster and trained it right on the awaking soldier. The barrel of the gun pushed up against the man's forehead so hard that it caused creases above his eyes. The man looked back into Burke's cold and terrified eyes with an equally shocked expression. The soldier's eyes quaked with terror and panic. There was even a slight shaking of his head, as if pleading with Burke and saying "No, please don't."

There, the two men looked at each other in dead silence for several excruciating seconds. Burke noticed that the look of fear in the soldier's eyes was the exact same look Leo gave him when they were first making their way out of the clearing near the crash site. It was the look that pleaded for death not to come today, however close death might be. Slowly, but gently, Burke began to lower his gun. Their gaze did not break, not even for a moment, and their faces remained steadfast and fixated in a look of terrified shock.

"I don't want to kill you," Burke whispered to him. "Please, oh God, please don't make me have to kill you. You understand?" he continued, shaking his head solemnly.

The man's face didn't change; Burke wasn't even sure if his message was getting through. Burke began slowly holstering his weapon, making his gun visible to the man so that the soldier knew what he meant.

"Please don't make me shoot at you," Burke reminded him, putting his finger up to his mouth as if to tell the soldier to "stay quiet." The soldier nodded, understanding. Burke then placed his hand over his own heart.

"Thank you," he said.

The man nodded again, still completely terrified. Outside, the soldier's roommate had finished his cigarette and was on his way back inside. Both men broke their gaze. The soldier was coming in.

"Ike," the man told Burke in an excited whisper, pointing to the rear entrance. "Ike!"

Burke jumped, with MRE's in hand, and bolted out the back of the tent. He raced back into the jungle, which welcomed him with open, dark, shadowy arms. Behind him, at the camp, there came a low chatter of voices, followed by a shout. Suddenly, there was a gunshot. Then another. A bullet tore through the trunk of a tree less than ten feet away from Burke. He had been spotted.

Dodging through the brush, John stumbled and hopped as quickly as he could, attempting to evade the soldier's bullets. Three, then four more shots fired at him with one of the rounds coming close to his knee. He reached at his hip, ready to return fire. As he went for his sidearm, the MRE's in his arms came tumbling out, rolling around everywhere on the ground. Burke knew that without an MRE, a bullet would bring death just the same as starvation would. He backtracked frantically a few feet before yet another bullet touched the ground and skidded off into the thick just to his right, bringing up leaves and debris and scattering them about in his face. The MREs, Burke decided, needed to be sacrificed.

Burke hobbled as fast as he could for another fifty yards. The lights from the soldiers who were closing in poked out towards him from the low-lying tree trunks and low-hanging branches all around. Suddenly, Burke felt his foot slip on a fallen tree branch, flinging his body straight onto the ground. His chin landed first, biting hard on the roof of his mouth and causing an instant headache. Clumsily, his sore body stumbled onto all fours. Unable to get back up on his feet,

Burke crawled behind a tree, his fingers tightly grasping the grip of his firearm. The lights grew closer. Orders came echoing from behind the light as soldiers barked aggressively at one another. They began to converge on his position; their lights were trained on the fallen tree Burke huddled behind. Enemy soldiers were not but ten yards away from Burke, armed with rifles and adrenaline. Burke sat there, sheltered poorly by the tree trunk, shaking and heaving like a mad man.

"Detekinasai!" the ultimatum rang.

It was the end. Burke counted a dozen shots in his clip and quickly loaded a bullet into place in the slide. From the rustling, he figured there were six, maybe seven men behind him. The odds were hard for him to calculate. If there were indeed six men, all with rifles, he would have to stand, shoot all six before they could get him, and race to pick up one of their rifles in case the other men from the camp were close behind. He would have to use every last bullet in his weapon to make a difference. It was then that the feeling of being trapped flooded over him; it was staggering. But Burke knew what he needed to do. His chips were down. The choice was made.

Burke tossed his weapon out from behind cover and his arms shot up. Slowly, he began to rise from behind the tree and face his captors. Their lights were pointed right at him making it hard, if not completely impossible, to see their faces. But Burke could see their rifles, and he could see that they were unflinchingly trained on him. The enemy didn't even give him the chance to see the whites of their eyes.

Suddenly, he felt a quick blow come swiftly to his lower back, which made him drop to his knees on all fours. He let it happen. There was nothing he could do but to let it happen. It was over. The brave man stayed behind and the coward stood up. He surrendered.

A boot of one of the soldiers came riding up hard and fast into Burke's ribcage. It lifted him off the ground and stole the air from his lungs. Then, the butt of a rifle came driving down onto his left shoulder blade and flattened him outright. The soldiers did this several times with intermittent kicks to his legs and knees. This went on for nearly a minute or so. As one soldier had a shot at him, another would come right up not even a full second later with another shot. Eventually, after they had effectively kicked all of Burke's optimism out, they stopped. Two of the soldiers grabbed him hard under the arm and started dragging him back to camp. Burke's limp body caught onto rocks and branches that seemed to reach out and try to hold him down. The soldiers just jerked on his body harder, ensuring that he would *not* get left behind.

When they had finally reached camp, the men who had remained behind had already prepared a place especially for Burke to stay that night. It was nothing more than a post in the ground, complete with sharp, steely cuffs. And before Burke could start enjoying the remote pleasure of warmth, another rifle butt dug into his belly and caused him to vomit both his MRE and any hope that he had left.

Several of the soldiers stayed up with their new house guest a moment longer to welcome him with berating remarks. Most of them eyeballed Burke from their respective place in the camp before going to their tents. All of the men made it very clear that they did not want him there any more than he wanted to be there. Unfortunately for both parties, they were stuck with each other until they received further orders. The night patrolmen kept an extra special set of eyes on Burke that night. One of them found a stool to sit on across from him and sat there hurling insults at Burke all night in Japanese. The other patrolman walked the perimeter carefully, occasionally checking on Burke as if hoping he would get the privilege of shooting the prisoner.

There was one soldier, though, who did not act so coldly. The sleeping man stood for quite some time at the mouth of his tent, gazing at Burke curiously. He still showed signs of shock and a bit of terror. Burke just looked back at the man pathetically, as if looking at him would help his bruising lung find a way to take in air again. The two exchanged sympathetic glances for some time. Eventually, the man retracted slowly into his tent and disappeared into the darkness of the room.

Through some miracle, Burke managed to close his eyes and go to sleep that night. It wasn't much and it wasn't good, but it was sleep nonetheless. In a way, it was more a passing out from exhaustion and pain.

The next morning, his aching body and stiff bones rattled him awake. He found it hard to move his neck much and his side was killing him from where they had first kicked him. Burke's feet were searing too, all the way up his knees. One of the soldiers came sauntering over, seeing that he was awake, and poked Burke hard in the side with his boot. Burke looked up at the man, who stared back at him down the barrel of a rifle.

"Okiru!" he grunted, motioning Burke to get up.

Burke looked down and realized that he had been unhooked from his post in the ground, but remained cuffed. A posse of three soldiers sat waiting impatiently for him in a jeep not far away. One of the soldiers, Burke noticed, was the sleeping man from the tent. He sat in the front of the jeep, looking back at Burke reassuringly. The other two made it clear they were put off and not eager to wait on him for anything. They yelled at him and motioned for him to come. From behind, the nose of a gun jabbed Burke hard underneath his rib cage and forced him forward. Burke climbed in the jeep and, before, he could even sit down all the way, they tore off down a dirt road. He stared at the camp as they made their way down the road and watched it slowly disappear from sight.

FIVE

Silently, they drove away from the camp with only the tumbling groans of the jeep's suspension to keep them company. Every few miles or so, one of the Japanese soldiers said a few words to the other, occasionally pointing off in the distance or scouring back at Burke. Not even the sleeping man said much to Burke, or even dared to look him in the eyes.

Erupting into view in the distance, a tall, beautiful mountain appeared from among the thick. It was covered in brown and red trees with speckled greenery among the mountain's floor. Low-lying clouds whipped and danced among the trees and birds soared in and out of the clouds. The image of the mountain looked as though it belonged on a postcard.

The jeep made its way alongside the mountain. As they entered, they were greeted with a dusting of leaves falling from the trees as though they were gently paving the way for them. Birds chirped and whistled delightful tunes from among the branches of the old, wise trees. It was strangely beautiful from all angles.

As they emerged over a ridge alongside the mountain, a very large encampment appeared. It was a stark contrast from the glory of the mountain; shiny, metal buildings and industrial equipment were scattered throughout the area and reflected the bright, rising sun off of their slick surfaces. The encampment faced north with nearly a hundred plus Japanese soldiers scurrying about their business. The more permanent buildings occupied the center of the encampment while makeshift tents and shanty shacks covered the perimeter. At the highest point of the camp was an incredibly large anti-aircraft gun; it was much larger than any Japanese artillery Burke had ever seen. The Americans had been shot at with typical ground fire and small AA cannons, which nearly every platoon in the war possessed; but never had they ever encountered an anti-aircraft gun of that magnitude before. It stuck out of the ground like a large trophy, standing with its giant nose to the sky full of pride. Suddenly Burke realized why the Air Force had them fly over the water and go back over the water instead of flying directly over the land during the Fukuoka run. The chilling thought came over him, *What if we actually made it over the island after the attack started.* He knew the answer – they would have been reduced to rubble by the outstretched arm of the Japanese AA.

The jeep pulled up straight through the center of the camp. None of the men paid any attention to their new prisoner; the soldiers in the camp kept themselves busy and motivated by things far more interesting than Burke. Finally, the jeep stopped, clear on the other side of the base near several old shanty shacks. From the overwhelming smell, Burke could tell that one of the shacks was a bathroom – or at least he hoped it was just a bathroom. The other shack didn't seem to smell much better, though. Quickly, the soldiers piled out of the jeep and two of them dragged Burke by the arms towards one of the shacks. The other soldier with them moseyed over to some of the other men who appeared to be stationed at the camp and began palling around with them, oblivious to his assigned reasons for being there. As the two soldiers dragging Burke drew closer to the shack, one of them suddenly dropped him on one side and went out ahead, unlocking the gate to the shack and flinging it open. Burke looked up at the soldier still grabbing him by the arm; it was the sleeping man. The soldier looked back at Burke sympathetically. The two only nodded their heads and slowly returned their gaze back to the middle distance.

The other soldier returned. He grabbed Burke hard underneath his arm and flung him forward, into the cell. Burke spilled out onto the dirt floor of the filthy shack. The room filled with the smell of waste and garbage. It was, however, slightly warmer than the frosty air outside, and Burke was thankful for this. Behind him, the door to the shack slammed shut and locked.

"Merry Christmas," said a dark voice from the corner of the room.

Burke shot up and saw a man, looking like he was in his mid-to-late thirties, covered in scruff and grime. His beard stuck out wildly in a hundred directions, covering his bony cheeks just enough to disguise his emaciation. He was dressed in what used to be green, standard issue fatigues, which had deteriorated into a faded, holey, dirt-stained mess.

"It is Christmas, right?" he asked.

Burke simply laid there on the floor, trying his best to get up under his own power. His side ached miserably from the boot heels of the soldiers and his neck was stiffer than a board.

"Guess you don't say much," the voice finally said, filling the silence.

"I-I'm sorry," Burke replied.

"What's your name, soldier? You are a soldier, correct?"

"Air Force. My name is Lieutenant John Burke."

"*Lieutenant* John Burke, eh? Aren't you a bit young to be a lieutenant?"

Burke nodded but didn't say a word.

The voice spoke up again. "I'm Major Andrew Lowrie, United States Navy. That's Corporal Ketch Harrison over there, also Navy," he said, nodding to the other corner of the room. "He was one of mine."

The other man in the room did not look much older than Burke: baby face, blonde hair, pale complexion. He was in slightly better looking shape than Major Lowrie but still possessed a weak frame beneath his baggy clothes. The Corporal kept his head to the ground, looking up sheepishly at their new guest.

"Where are you from?" Burke asked him, hoping to get him to talk.

"Wichita Falls. How'd you become a lieutenant?" he replied quickly.

"Beg your pardon?"

"You're not much older than me, so how'd you become a lieutenant?" he shot back.

Burke shook his head and gave a crooked smile. "Luck, I guess."

"Guess your luck ran out too," Harrison replied.

Major Lowrie got up and started towards Burke. "Come on, get to your feet, soldier," he said, helping him up off the floor. "Don't mind him, it's been a long few weeks."

"How long have you been here?" Burke asked him.

"Going on twenty weeks," Lowrie replied. "We got whittled down to only a few men during a skirmish by Kolombangara in the Solomons back in July. The few of us who jumped ship made our way to the island shores. Corporal Harrison and I got picked up on Kolombangara while trying to make it to central New Georgia. Been here ever since."

"Was it just the two of you?" Burke asked.

"From that battle, yes. They didn't take many prisoners. We got lucky. Once we got picked up we got sent to Japan pretty quickly. First to some place in the Nagasaki province and then on up here."

Burke rubbed his head, which had maintained a constant and dull headache since he had landed, and looked around the room, attempting to gain his bearings. It was a dark space, save for a light that came in through a small, barred window at the top of the wall.

The window was barely large enough for a rat to crawl through, but from the rat feces on the ground, Burke assumed they still managed to find a way in. There was nothing on the walls and nothing on the ground; it was bare empty except for a hole in one corner of the room for "business matters." Under the window, a dark, silhouetted figure was curled up in a ball on the ground. The shadow did not move or budge, but lay there with his back to the others, facing the wall.

"You said before you came here, you were in Nagasaki," Burke asked Lowrie and Harrison. "So where is 'here' exactly?"

Corporal Harrison sat up. "Mount Sefuri in the Sawara Ward of Japan," he stated with authority.

"At least we think that's where we are," Major Lowrie added. "We aren't sure but we've heard some of the soldiers talk about a set-up in Fukuoka, so we figured we are somewhere around there."

"I was just in Fukuoka," Burke replied.

"How was the weather?" Lowrie said with a smile. The joke was lost on Burke, who was preoccupied, attempting to map out where he was exactly.

"What were you doing in Fukuoka?" Corporal Harrison asked.

"I was sent on a bombing run there... That's where I got shot d... got shot down." The words came surprisingly hard for Burke as thoughts of Leo, Lucky, and the others came to his mind.

"When was this?" Harrison responded quickly, bringing Burke back to focus.

"A couple days ago."

"Wait, so they know you went down!?" Harrison questioned excitedly.

"Yeah, I'm sure they do," Burke said, still thinking about his squad mates.

"Corporal…" Major Lowrie inserted.

The corporal continued on in an eager rant. "They know where you are, right? They can send help?"

"Corporal, don't do this to yourself…" said Lowrie.

"They can come get us! They know where we are!" Harrison shouted at the major, smiling wide from ear to ear.

Major Lowrie turned to Burke, ignoring the corporal. "Did you radio in after the crash?"

"No," Burke responded.

"How many of you survived?"

"There were only two of us who made it to the ground. Leo die… the other pilot died yesterday morning."

"So it's just you?" he continued.

"Yes."

Lowrie ducked his head and stirred up dust with the balls of his feet. "So they probably won't send a search team," he said to himself. "They aren't coming."

Harrison's excitement was still stirring him with enthusiasm and prayers of thanksgiving. The major, somberly, tried to calm the kid's excitement and get his attention.

"Corporal, they aren't coming," he told Harrison. The kid didn't listen. "They aren't coming," Lowrie kept repeating, louder and louder.

He finally grabbed Harrison's attention. The looks of excitement quickly turned to looks of anger and doubt. Defiantly he began to push the major away and argue. "They'll come!" he shouted. "They're coming, I know it!"

Finally, Major Lowrie won out. Raising his voice as loud as he could he shouted, "They aren't coming!" There was a silence between the men as the room filled with tenseness. "We've been here too long, son," Lowrie said.

The room grew still with disappointment. Burke wanted to change the subject as quickly as he could; he gained no comfort in Major Lowrie's words either. Harrison had sunk back to the ground in silent tears. Much longer and Burke might have done likewise. He looked around the empty room, searching for something to say. The dark figure on the ground below the window still had not moved since Burke had entered. "Who is he?" Burke asked quickly.

Major Lowrie shifted a glance to the figure on the ground. "That's Sergeant Millson. Marines. He doesn't say anything."

"Well, how long has he been here?" Burke asked.

"Before me and Harrison. He doesn't say anything, though."

John looked at Millson, who stirred only once. "How did they find him?"

"What did I say? He doesn't say anything," Lowrie responded. Realizing his brashness, he continued, "My best guess is they found him just the way you see him now." Major Lowrie made his way back to his mound on the ground on the other side of the room. He bent his head down and started picking nervously at his fingernails. "So is it really Christmas?" he grumbled.

"No," John finally responded. "It's still about a week away."

Lowrie merely nodded his head and continued picking at his fingernails. It was a wonder he had any at all. Burke quickly learned that in truth, Lowrie was a quiet man. None of the men talked much to each other, especially Millson who in fact did not speak at all. When the other men did talk, they found themselves sharing more about their personal lives than any of them had done while stationed on the mainland. Somehow, talking about family or friends or love interests back home, whether good or bad, helped remind them that they still had lives somewhere.

Lowrie impressed Burke the most. He never seemed very hopeful, yet somehow he managed to hold onto some hope deep within himself. Any time either Burke or Harrison began dreaming about hope, Lowrie squelched their conversation quickly. He never wanted any of them to feel too sure about anything. The truth was, Burke was surprised that Lowie wasn't the most hopeful one there. Back in the States, Lowrie had a wife and two kids waiting in Nebraska for him. He had a dog, a good job, and a good church with wholesome neighbors. Major Lowrie was a good American too, who enlisted in the military himself without considering waiting for the draft. He had served a short stint in Europe before being shipped to float around in the Pacific shortly after Pearl Harbor. He *earned* his rank, earned the respect he got from his men, and did a damn fine job serving his country. From the stories he told, and the few that Corporal Harrison told of him, Lowrie was a fierce and unyielding soldier at his post. Burke imagined that if he had met Major Lowrie anywhere outside their prison, he would remind him an awful lot of Hector. The big difference between him and Hector, of course, was that Major Lowrie did not have the same look in his eye that Hector did. He had all the balls that Hector had, just with more brains, more patience.

Corporal Harrison rarely got involved in lengthy conversations with Lowrie or Burke. When he did talk, it was usually only a few sentences before he went back to either sulking or yearning for freedom. As it turned out, Corporal Harrison was from Illinois, not even a hundred miles from Burke's hometown. Beyond that, however, the two men shared little in common. Corporal Harrison, unlike Lowrie, held onto hope wherever he could find it, although hope was rarely found. If there was ever a buzz about the camp outside, or a storm front that came in from a different direction than it had come before, Harrison figured freedom was right around the corner. When the euphoria of hope had dissipated, Harrison mostly brooded to himself and looked out the window at the sky, waiting for salvation.

Of course, Sergeant Millson did not say much of anything. In fact, he said nothing. Ever. At first, this worried John. If Millson wasn't lying on the ground under the window completely mute, he was hunkered over, staring out the window at the hillside behind the shack completely mute. John attempted to make conversation with him at times during his first week. Millson would occasionally reply by cocking his head slightly before shrinking back into himself. Once, and only once, did Millson ever clear his throat. His voice sounded deep and charred, as if he had swallowed a handful of gravel. Beyond that moment, he did not make a peep.

As time dragged on, the initial worry John harbored towards him turned into being perplexed. John realized he had no idea why it was that Millson said nothing for so long. The kind of commitment it took for Millson to say nothing for that long was, by itself, something to respect. It took bones of steel to stay that secluded for so long. Eventually, over time, Burke realized why Sergeant Millson did not say anything. He realized that it was the same reason neither he, nor Harrison or Lowrie talked to one another for very long. Sergeant Millson said nothing probably because there was nothing really left to be said. If there were something worth saying, it would have been said. The sergeant just never quite found the words important enough to say to the rest of them.

It was a hard concept for John to imagine. As a man who found no few subjects to talk about at length later on in life, he strangely found that the sort of silence he experienced those days in prison made sense. It seemed without fail, in his older years, that one of his kids would ask him to tell stories about his life during the war, usually around Veteran's Day. John mostly told them stories like the time he was covered in leeches or the time he was hospitalized on base because the doctor was poisoning him. On rare occasion would he say anything about being shot out of the sky or something about a bombing run. These stories were *extremely* rare. But the one thing John never said much about, if he said anything at all, was about life inside the cell. It wasn't because he didn't *want* to talk about it. He never said anything about it because he didn't have anything *to* say about it, good or bad. Life in the cell was as follows: sleep, eat two rations of raw fish a day, vomit, go to bed. At first it seemed horrible, but after doing it two hundred seventy-nine times in a row, John began to understand why there was nothing to really say.

For Burke, the worst part of being imprisoned wasn't being treated cruelly, getting kicked in the gut, being slandered, or even being utterly degraded in every sense of the word. He endured all of those things back home in Illinois *before* he joined the war. The worst part of being imprisoned, to him, was being allowed to do the same thing, over and over and over again, until things eventually began to lose meaning altogether. Burke only had to repeat his day of doing nothing for two hundred seventy-nine days. As John later found out, Sergeant Millson did it five hundred fifty-seven times. Burke imagined that around the four hundredth time, it finally worked. Imprisonment finally stripped the words and meaning out of living completely.

Six months after John arrived at the camp, Sergeant Millson came down with a cold. His cold turned into a wheezing cough. The wheezing cough eventually became a scorching fever. Through the whole process, Millson never said a word. He spent his days looking out the window or staring at the wall, all five hundred and fifty-seven days. Eventually, in June of 1944, Sergeant Millson gave up the grave as quietly as the others had always known him to be. Guards came in and dragged his body out of room, burying him in a nameless grave outside of the camp.

Even though the others were there when Sergeant Millson died, none of them knew what his last words were – they were spoken long before they had arrived there. The truth was, his life outlived his living. By the time he finally died, there was nothing really left to say that hadn't already been said, and there hadn't been something to say for months.

SIX

The last thing Lieutenant Burke remembered about the prison camp where he was imprisoned were leaves. They were everywhere. He hated leaves. The trees along the hillside outside their window turned incredible shades of reds, browns, yellows, and oranges. Looking outside the window of the shack, they could only see a short way up the hill. The mountainside blocked most of the view from them, but they at least had the minor pleasure of seeing a few trees turn.

Leaves from every inch of the island blew in through their window. They were beautiful at first but quickly turned brown and began composting on their floor. Burke spent some of his days just gathering up what leaves blew in and shoving them back out through the bars of the window. It was a crummy sort of entertainment, but it was something.

Things were getting quieter too. Over time, the three of them – Corporal Harrison, Major Lowrie, and Lieutenant Burke – all started running out of things to even think about. Somehow the lack of Sergeant Millson's presence made the room even quieter. The guards who threw food in at them twice a day rarely said anything more than a grunt to anyone and the rest of the camp was usually too preoccupied with menial tasks here and there to notice the prisoner's presence among them.

Despite Burke never being a religious man, he often wished he had been able to have his Bible so that he would at least have something to read. Somewhere in between his surrender and his imprisonment, his Bible had been taken or lost. He desperately wished he had it, though. All he could remember from the good book was the bit about a God being over the deep of the waters and a few parables here and there, though he could never remember how they ended. He did occasionally talk to God, though never out loud. He often asked God what the purpose of the imprisonment was all about; he never got a response. By the time the doors did open on his cell, Burke figured all God ever wanted him to do was to shut up, and God succeeding in doing so, for a time anyways.

John Burke lived in that prison from December of 1943 to October of 1944. He heard nothing about the war, nothing about America, and nothing about his hometown during that period of time. He even had a hard time figuring out what month it was. No one came in to stay with them and no one left that room without dying. By the time their escape had finally come, the three men had hit their first week of complete and total silence together.

Around twilight, as the leaves began to change colors with the arrival of autumn, a faint din came rolling in from the distant horizon. It was the first sound any of them had heard all day. The noise started off as a hum, no louder than a whisper. It grew slowly into a buzz. The buzzing eventually became a growl from up above in the sky. While the other two men did not move an inch, Burke slowly raised his head and gazed at the changing, bright sky through their window. He knew the sound well. It was the first time he had ever really heard it closing in from the ground before. Soon, all three men took note of the sound and slowly looked at each other as it grew closer.

"I hear it too," Major Lowrie confirmed.

"Do you think…?" Corporal Harrison asked.

"Check it out," Lowrie ordered.

Harrison got up quickly and peeked out the window. "I can't see anything," he said. Suddenly, the soldiers outside the shack began to shuffle and scurry, loudly yelling orders at each other.

"I know what it is," Burke announced.

The other men darted their gaze at him. "Is it them?" the corporal asked.

Burke shut his eyes and listened intently to the chatter of the soldiers on the other side of the wall. There was a lot of commotion, the chatter and frantic paces of the soldiers growing increasingly more concerned. Burke nodded to Corporal Harrison. It was them.

"They're coming," Harrison said to himself. "They're coming! They're coming!" Harrison began darting around the room and shouting with excitement.

"Are you sure it's them?" Major Lowrie asked the lieutenant. Burke nodded. "They found us? They know we're here?"

Corporal Harrison grabbed Major Lowrie by the shoulders and began shaking him excitedly, still chanting a hymn of salvation and dancing wildly. Even Lowrie began to smile. "Maybe it's over," he said to himself. "It could be over by now."

The grumble of the engines grew closer. They turned quickly into almost an all-out roar. Burke was not smiling; it was not over, not by a long shot. "No," Burke told them. "It isn't over; those planes don't stop. We don't make stops."

Major Lowrie looked back at Burke, puzzled, searching for an explanation. John didn't have time to give one. The whistle of the first package's free fall had already begun. Another whistle joined in. Then another. Suddenly a blast exploded out of an AA gun nearby. It had started.

The first detonation blew all three men down to the ground. It had hit on the other side of the camp, but the impact of the shockwave was enough to knock them down. Then another impact, a little closer, jostled them around the floor of the shack. Burke screamed for the others to get in the corner and cover their heads as he slid against the wall and brought his hands up as a shield. Four more impacts shook them and kicked them around a little while longer. The ringing in their ears was unbearable.

After a minute of hearing the bombs drop, Lieutenant Burke poked his head up from his place in the corner and looked towards the door of the shack. It was hanging wide open; the entire front side of the shack had been bent over backwards during the blast and was lying in a mangled mess all around them. Somehow, only the doorframe remained.

Outside, the camp was in a terrible commotion. With the bombs they had dropped, Burke figured there would have been no camp at all to see. There should have been a crater, or even level ground. Instead, the area was burning with bright red and orange flames lapping up at a purple, twilight sky. The trees around the camp that had just changed colors were soon engulfed in wild flames as well; flames that turned the bark on the trees a charred, empty black. A few men were still running around the camp, their silhouettes dancing against the backdrop of the fire underneath the purple sky. These were not the same bombs they had been using before. These bombs were different. They were firebombs. As they hit, a blaze shot out from underneath them and set fire to anything that was around it. They didn't blow *up,* they blew *out.*

Frantically, the three men stood up. None of them had any idea what their next move would be, but they knew they needed to get out quickly. The surviving soldiers in the camp were running like mad, either to escape the flames or to load their weapons and aim for the skies; not a single eye paid attention to the three, scrawny prisoners.

"We have to get out of here!" Lowrie shouted. Harrison and Burke nodded and took off behind him into the camp. All around them, buildings and tents were being engulfed into one, massive inferno. The stench of chemicals from the bombs burned their eyes and noses, while even the surface of their skin grew tight and hot. Charred bodies lay on the ground all around them; they were the most gruesome sight Burke had *ever* seen in his life. The sight and smell of the bodies stayed with him and even the thought of them made him nauseous. It was a feeling he never forgot.

Major Lowrie stopped running right before making it to the open road that went directly through the middle of the camp, waiting for the others to catch up. "We need to make it into the woods!" he shouted over the roars of the fire. "Do NOT split up; we need to stick together. Corporal Harrison, I think I saw a jeep on the other side of this road. I'll run over with you and we will start it up. Lieutenant Burke – follow us until you get over to that tent right in front of the jeep. You run in and see if you can find supplies for us and meet us out by the jeep ASAP. Got it?"

Harrison and Burke nodded. Lowrie examined the road in either direction and gave them the signal to move. Immediately, the three made a beeline across the road as fast as they could. Down at the other side of the camp, gunshots flung up into the sky at the planes overhead. The metal birds swung up high and began their flip, returning home. The massive anti-aircraft gun in the center of the base sat in a crumbling, twisted heap of metal.

The three men made it to the tent in front of the jeep. Lowrie and Harrison went on ahead of Burke to the vehicle as Burke ducked inside the tent. There wasn't much in the tiny space; it looked like a barrack of some sort. On the wall were medical supplies, which Burke swiped quickly, along with a blanket at the foot of the bed.

Underneath the bed, Burke shuffled through books, dirty pictures, and other assorted junk, flinging them out into the space violently. Suddenly, he ran across the butt of a rifle. He brought it out and checked the chamber – no bullets, and there were none to be found. Burke took it anyway, thinking it might still come in handy for something. As he stood up, taking what little he had with him clumsily in his arms, a voice shouted at him to his right. It was followed by the familiar click of a safety on a rifle.

"*Tate!*" said the voice. Burke slowly rose and turned. A Japanese soldier stood there, trembling fearfully on the other end of a loaded rifle. The man looked familiar. The two of them stood quietly gazing at the other. It was the sleeping man who had escorted Burke to the camp upon his capture.

"Let me go," Burke pleaded, offering the man his rifle as a sign of peace. "Please, don't make me go back. Please…"

The soldier stood his ground for a moment. The fear in his pupils made his whole body quake, and over the roar of the fire outside the tent, it was almost impossible to hear each other. As Burke spoke, though, the man began to relax, his eyes widening. He realized who he was pointing his gun at. It was then Burke said one of the only Japanese words he knew, something he had learned from the military handbook given to him at Guadalcanal. "Kudasai, please. *Kudasai.*"

"Wakatta," he replied. The soldier nodded and slowly lowered his weapon.

Suddenly, the side of the tent towards the entrance caught fire. The flames began to climb over their heads quickly.

"Ike!" he screamed, pointing to the rear entrance. "Deteike, ike ike!"

Burke nodded and ran out of the tent. He never saw the sleeping man come out; in his heart, he prayed that he made it out alive.

Major Lowrie and the corporal already had the jeep running. Harrison was at the wheel with Lowrie bent over the back of the jeep waving Burke in. "Hurry up!" he screamed.

Burke halfway tossed the medical supplies and blanket into the back of the jeep and handed the rifle over to Lowrie in the passenger's side. "No bullets," Burke explained, climbing in himself.

"No worries. Take us out of here, Harrison, move!"

Harrison floored the jeep and hurdled towards the main road. Dirt and ash flew as he dug the tires into the ground and turned away from the camp. The uneven road jogged the men up and down like a bobber lure in a trout pond. Burke twisted around in the back and stared at the Japanese camp, taking it into full view as they drove away. Fire was everywhere. It looked like Sodom and Gomorrah, hell from the heavens. In the lavender sky, all six planes flew back towards the Pacific. The screams of the men suffering the fires of the camp rose above the scorching flames. Every building was ablaze; even the shack in which the men had lived every day of their lives together for the past ten months had turned into nothing more than ash. As they drove away, Burke could see the whole camp better. He saw things he wished he hadn't. The image of the camp penetrated the deepest parts of his mind and tattooed itself there. Even as they drove down the hillside and the camp disappeared from site, the image remained.

There were many terrifying images Burke had after the war. None were more terrifying than the image of the firebombing. He never spoke of the things he saw to anyone, and he never wanted to so that no one else would gain a picture of the atrocities. But nonetheless, it was the single most gruesome memory Burke had of the war, and it never went away. They had taken their bombs, which already effectively turned life into death in the first place, and had made the damned things breathe fire. Burke shook his head, tears rolling down his cheek and nose, thinking *how could it get any worse than this?* He wondered what more they could do to make war even uglier than it already was. Somehow, they did, though. By the end of the war, they would have made it something much, much worse.

Harrison drove them away from the blaze and into the jungle. As they went deeper and deeper into the trees, the air grew colder and the sky turned from violet to black. Even as they entered the darkness, the orange glow of the camp emanated from the hillside to the north. They eventually came to a stop near a stream not far from the road, some eight miles from the camp at Mount Sefuri. The three men piled out of the vehicle and gathered themselves as best they could.

Major Lowrie quickly put them on track. "We will have the best luck if we head for open water and hitch a ride. The closest port is Nagasaki, which is out of the question. Too congested. We will aim southeast and get into open waters, which will give us a straight shot for the Solomon's or at least the Philippines... I hope to God we make it that far..."

As Lowrie continued, Burke found himself drawn to the glow of the fire to the east. It was an eerie sight, watching what used to be their prison and what could have been their grave burn to the ground. There were men still there, people who were dying in ways he could not have imagined before. Pilots never saw the faces of the men they killed. They only heard the pop of the explosive on the ground as they gently sailed back home. The images of men dying in the flames on the Japanese base haunted Burke because he finally saw the faces of the men who died underneath his plane.

I helped do that he thought, and he did not like the thought at all.

"Lieutenant Burke," Major Lowrie asserted. "We need you here, are you with us?"

Burke did a double take and looked back at him. "I am, sorry," he replied.

"Lieutenant, we need you here. The only way we will make it to the coast and off this island is if we stay together, got it? We don't have long. We need to get out of here before the men from that mountain start scattering all around here. Let's take a few minutes to regroup and get our bearings and then get out of here."

Harrison and Burke agreed with a nod.

"Are we really going to get out of here?" Corporal Harrison asked Major Lowrie.

Lowrie paused for a moment and searched the ground with his eyes for an answer. Carefully, cautiously, Lowrie looked up at both of the men and with a determined gaze in his eyes stated, "Yeah. Yeah, we're getting out of here."

SEVEN

The three drove quietly through the jungle at a snail's pace all night. It was a cold night and the temperature only dropped as wind whipped past them sidelong. The blanket Burke snatched took turns warming each man as they drove down winding paths, off road, through muddy streams, and right through the heart of nowhere. After a while, the rows and rows of dense trees and foliage grew old. Several times the men would have to stop the jeep and push it out of a rut or would have to wait for Japanese patrols to pass in front of them. All in all, the two hundred mile journey took them a total of eight hours to complete.

It was early morning when they neared the coast; it was almost 0800. The familiar smell of ocean water snagged their attention; the shore was close. Harrison pushed the jeep a little faster, excited by the smell of salt and freedom. Tree after tree, shrub and bush, whizzed past them as Harrison tossed and weaved the vehicle through the jungle.

Suddenly, they broke from the thick into a wide-open field. Beneath their tires, rice plants ironed flat and were ground into tiny bits. Out in front of the men, nearly a hundred yards, were workers – two women and one child – whose attention was immediately drawn away from picking rice and directed quickly towards the jeep. The women stood their ground in the field while the child darted away and began shouting towards a small village on the outskirts of the field.

"Slow down," Major Lowrie barked at Harrison. "Aim for the road over there, let's get off their rice patty."

Harrison took the jeep out of the field and onto a road not thirty yards away. At the end of the road was a small, desolate village. There were no flags waving above any of the buildings, and it seemed stripped and bare of any weapons or artillery. In fact, as they drove through, Burke noticed not a single young man in all the village. There were a few men who were old and frail, or missing limbs, but there were certainly no fighting men to be seen. The buildings in the village were in bad shape too. They resembled the shanty shack where the three men had lived in for so long either. A few of the buildings were raised off of the ground and were constructed of stone or cheap wood. They were far from extravagant, by any means. As they drove through the village center, women and children began poking their heads out of windows and doorframes while a few spilled onto the streets to watch them pass by. Harrison slowed the vehicle down to little more than a crawl; the sound of small rocks and dirt crunching beneath their tires echoed throughout the village.

"Should we be worried?" Harrison asked.

"Why should we be worried?" Major Lowrie replied.

"They're Japs, sir."

"They're only looking at us, Corporal."

"Why aren't there soldiers here?" Burke asked.

Lowrie examined the town. There wasn't much to speak of in the village and the overgrowth of mangled earth and plant life outside the perimeter was virtually unlivable. "There's nothing here," Lowrie replied. "They've got crappy rice patties and a helluva view of nothing. The men are somewhere far more important than here."

Harrison kept rolling past the sad eyes and forlorn stares of the villagers. Their faces were tired, some even emaciated, and the village smelled of disease. The men fell silent. Lieutenant Burke thought he heard Lowrie speak under his breath once, though: "Poor are always poor."

They neared the end of the village. Lowrie stood up in his seat to try and see over the horizon to where they were going. The jungle made it hard to see much of any path in front of them and Lowrie motioned for Harrison to come to a stop.

"We need to find a boat of some kind," he said, still staring off, examining the path through the thick. "I can't see a whole hell of a lot here; maybe one of the villagers has a leftover fishing vessel we can use." Lowrie jumped out of the car, taking the map with him, and began approaching the villagers. Harrison looked quizzically at Burke, who shrugged and suggested that he pull over.

Harrison pulled up alongside a group of thin, Japanese women who had clustered together on the side of the road. They looked as though they were in their forties, even early fifties, Burke thought. None of the women said a word and few of them made eye contact with them. Back on the road, Major Lowrie was pointing at a map and fumbling through a few Japanese words that he remembered with a group of mothers and their young children. Harrison quickly dodged over to Lowrie and began dancing around him, keeping an eye out for any unwelcomed company. From the look of the conversation Lowrie was having, it was not going well. Harrison offered little help, as well. Lowrie mostly shook his head and kept saying "Nami" which meant "wave" in Japanese, then he would make a wave sound and point down to the map. In reply, one of the women would wave at Lowrie nervously and look down at the map. Beside them, a group of eleven-year old boys were teasing and laughing at the American who grew more and more frustrated with the woman who kept waving at him when he said "wave." Burke smiled to himself and decided it was best to leave them up to their own devices to figure it out.

"Ask them where 'Nami' is!" Corporal Harrison kept telling Lowrie.

"What the hell do you think I'm doing?" Lowrie shot back.

Meanwhile, the woman they were talking to kept waving at them sheepishly. The young boys nearby only laughed harder.

"Ah, screw it," grumbled Lowrie, giving up on his Japanese. "Where is a boat!? Water? We want ocean and boat. Where is ocean and boat?" Lowrie kept saying it louder and louder in English, as if it were suddenly going to click for them.

"Nami! We want Nami, dammit!" Harrison shouted nervously. The woman continued waving at him, then turned, and ran back into the house letting out a scared whimper as she did. The other women said nothing and passively ignored her frustration. The young boys nearby howled in laughter.

Burke shook his head and sauntered away from the frustrating language barrier. He didn't speak much Japanese, if really any, and didn't want to offer his opinion on the matter. He knew just enough to eat and keep his butt clean and he didn't really feel like he needed to know more.

Leaving Harrison and Lowrie to do their arguing by themselves, John swung his feet out over the back of the jeep and plopped himself onto the ground. He began to wander around the village, looking casually into the doorways of the huts. Inside, the homes were stark naked. Nothing hung from the wall. There were no cabinets or countertops. There was nothing. Without going in, Burke could see a few beds made out of linens and what looked like grass. They were crummy little cots, not much better than the provisions they had in prison. The villagers were people who had little to nothing to live for, yet somehow found a way to keep on living in spite of it.

We probably bombed their family and friends Burke thought to himself. The thought stopped him. These people were not only experiencing the effects of the war from the Americans, but were forgotten about by their own people, left in their "crummy rice patty" to live by themselves in solitude. And there they lived, and somehow survived.

Behind him, Lowrie and Harrison were still making the young boys of the village laugh with their poor grasp of the Japanese language. One of the teenage boys eventually stepped forward and spoke a few words in English, trying to convey messages to the men one word at a time. Burke snuffed out an amused smile and headed back to the jeep. It didn't feel right to leave the people alone like they were without telling them what was coming for them, he thought; and it certainly didn't feel right to take their boats and abandon them on the island without refuge or any means of escape. More bombs were sure to come and more fighting was right at their doorstep. John didn't know what good it would have done to warn them, but it certainly didn't feel right to leave them alone. He knew what it felt like to be caught in the middle of darkness without anyone there to help – it was like he felt the morning that Leo passed away. Like the villagers, he was left *alone*, in the middle of a fight he never wanted to be a part of in the first place.

As he leaned up against the jeep, a young boy came hurdling towards him and hit him right in the stomach. The boy was no more than nine years old, in good shape, pitch-black straight hair, and had a funny looking freckle right below his left eye. The boy looked up sheepishly at Burke and quickly hid his head from him when they made eye contact. Burke smiled and pushed him back, brushing the dust off of him. He bent down and met the boy's eyes, smiling. The two stood there awkwardly looking at each other for a long time; the boy danced around, wanting to say something but not able to get it out.

"Kon'nichiwa," Burke said to him with a little wave from the hip.

The kid grinned and dodged his eyes up at Burke quickly. "Kon'nichiwa," he squeaked out.

"My name is John. *John*. John – that's me," he said, pointing to himself. "What is your name?" he continued, pointing at the boy. The boy looked unsure. "*John*. Me, John. You?"

The kid finally gave a nod, understanding, and replied, "Watashi no namae wa Kioshi desu."

"Kioshi?" John confirmed. The boy nodded. "Kioshi. That's a great name, Kioshi."

Over at the jeep, Burke noticed that Lowrie and Harrison were finally fighting over how to accurately say "thank you" in Japanese while the young boys nearby cackled at them madly. He began to move to get into the jeep and leave.

Kioshi tugged at the hem of John's shirt. "Watashi wa anata to issho ni kuru koto ga dekiru?"

John shook his head. "I'm sorry, I don't understand." Kioshi repeated himself again, saying "Anata to" several times emphatically and pointing to Burke.

"Me?" John said. "I'm sorry kid, I don't understand Japanese."

Kioshi, again, repeated "Anata to" and pointed even more ferociously at John and then at the jeep.

"Anata to?..." Burke uttered. "...come with? You want to come with me? Is that what you're asking?" The boy looked back eagerly. "I'm sorry, you can't come with us. No. No Anata to. Sorry." Kioshi continued to beg, eagerly tugging at Burke's arm and returning in even closer as Burke would push him away.

"Hey lieutenant," Major Lowrie shouted at Burke from the jeep. Lowrie and Harrison managed to relieve themselves of interpreting and were ready and waiting. "I think we found the place we were looking for, we're rolling out."

"Yeah okay, give me a second." Burke replied with Kioshi still at his heels. Burke turned, crouched down, and took Kioshi by the shoulders. "Look, kid. Kioshi. I can't take you, you can't come. You don't want to come, okay?"

Kioshi just looked back at him with deep, sad eyes.

"I'm sorry, really, I am." John's heart sunk. Deep within the gaze of that child was a fear of being left alone that John knew all too well. In his own heart, John wanted to give the boy something, anything he could, so that the boy could keep a piece of him. John searched his pants and pockets and found nothing. "I'm sorry, I don't have anything," he said.

The boy just looked back at Burke, smiling eagerly. Burke smiled back.

"Hurry up, lieutenant, we need to go!" Lowrie barked.

Burke patted the boy's head and smiled once more at him. "Take care, alright?" he told Kioshi, getting up and jumping into the jeep.

"Looks like there might be a boat down a ways to the south," Lowrie briefed him. "We're going to head to the coast and follow it until we see something."

Harrison quickly pulled out and headed down the road. Some of the older boys, who had spent much of their time teasing the American men on their Japanese, ran alongside the vehicle while the women stayed behind and looked about as clueless about the three men's intentions as when they got there.

"Ariga-*toe*!" Harrison shouted as he waved to the women.

"It's Ariga-too, Harrison," Major Lowrie corrected.

"I'm telling you, it's Ariga-toe," Harrison shot back.

"You're impossible, son."

"At least I know my Japanese. I wasn't deaf in that camp, you know. I picked up a few words."

"Few words my ass…"

The two began to argue back and forth. Burke shook his head in agitation and turned back in his seat to take another look at the village as it disappeared from site. The huts and homes looked as though they all leaned away from each other. Light from the morning sun poked out through open slats and holes in the exterior walls. The teenage boys who helped interpret continued to run a ways behind their jeep before slowly tapering off. The women had since dispersed, no doubt unimpressed with the "American intellect." Lastly, Burke saw little Kioshi, doddling around right where he had left him. He looked up as the men drove off. He looked miserable, longing to come with them to wherever it was they were going, with the hopes that wherever it was, it was better.

"I'm sorry, kid," Burke said to himself. "I know the feeling."

Eventually, the village got lost as they drove into more trees and the laughter of the young boys faded away to the sound of Lowrie and Harrison's arguing. The three men were almost in the home stretch and were almost off the island for good.

EIGHT

In total, Burke had spent almost an entire year in Japan before seeing the "Rising Sun" with his own two eyes. When he finally did, it was incredibly underwhelming at first. As Burke grew older and eventually moved to New Mexico, he would see the sky streak with purples and oranges and reds virtually every night at *sunset*. The sunset was one of his favorite parts of living in the southwest; the sky became virtually a canvas of paints that were delicately streaked among the fluffy clouds. In Japan, however, the sunset was nothing more than a pale yellow ball falling out of the sky which came across as altogether uninteresting. But as they drove towards the beach early in the morning to secure a boat and head off over the dark, empty sea, Burke caught a glimpse of the infamous Rising Sun. It was unlike anything he had ever seen. It looked as though the sun had shot down over the water with rays of mist and dew scattering particles about all around it. The light came over the earth gently and reached out to them with its arms wide open. It was the most beautiful thing John ever saw the sky create.

When he looked at his Japanese flag every morning at breakfast, John would catch himself laughing on the inside at the thought of it being red. He never knew why they chose the color red for the sun in the center of the flag. In reality, the sun came up a soft orange and yellow color. Right after the war ended, some Americans looked at the center of a Japanese flag and seemed to imagine the people as a group of damned barbarians or vicious, uneducated beasts; it was as if the Japanese painted their flag with the blood of their enemies or something. Burke saw it differently. He loved the sunrise over Japan. It was amazing, even though it looked nothing like the flag. Granted, he never wanted to live in Japan and after getting off the island, he never wanted to go back. But the truth was he deeply respected the country and its people. He was, of course, part of a team of people who sent bombs to the island on a daily basis, thousands upon thousands of bombs, and blew the place sky high, turning it essentially into an ashtray. Every morning, though, the people of Japan still woke up and looked at that beautiful yellow sun, waiting for it to turn red as the planes rolled in carrying death on board. And they did this every day.

While he didn't know why the flag was painted with a red sun, Burke came up with his own theories. After spending a few months on the island during the war, John no longer came to see the sun over Japan as a source of light. He saw it, like many there, as a big red spotlight for the bombing planes to aim for, as if the sun illuminated Japan as a target. While he lived on Guadalcanal, John would occasionally hear some of the men say that the red sun on the

Japanese flag gave them something to aim with – made Japan a great target for their reticule. When he looked back at this thought, it always made him think of Lucky, as he crashed into the side of a fighter vessel. Burke could just imagine the sight of the big red Japanese flag coming at Lucky quickly, illuminating his path as he barreled towards the ship. It was a terrifying thought.

From what Burke remembered, Lucky never talked about the Japanese flag, Japanese people, or anything to do with the country itself. Lucky certainly never liked talking about the missions either. If Hector ever went too far with a joke about the Japanese, in fact, Lucky would either shut him up or simply leave. Burke always thought that if he could ask Lucky what he really thought about the Japanese or the war, he liked to think that Lucky might have agreed with him on some things. At least he knew that Lucky respected the people, just as Burke did. At least, as Burke eventually did.

Burke looked at the Japanese flag, with its big red sun, the same way he looked at Lucky's scars across his face. Lucky had memories in his scars. The Japanese also had memories in their scars. Lucky and the Japs seemed to share a common bond – they had both been scarred. The Japanese people respected their scarred land the same way Lucky respected his scars with a cigarette. Burke remembered Lucky's cigarette ritual distinctly. Lucky would take out a cigarette from his pocket, bring it to his lips, and right before lighting it, he would rub the scars around his mouth with his thumbs ever so gently. It was as if Lucky was remembering how and why he got the scars he did. They were scars in the perfect shape of a broken beer bottle that didn't need to be there. They were scars that he sometimes egged on to get and other times did nothing to deserve. In any form, they were there, and they were not forgotten.

Lucky's scars reminded him of what he suffered to get to where he was in the first place. His scars reminded him of the evil in this world and in himself. It was the same type of memory that Burke always noticed in the Rising Sun of the Japanese flag. The sunrise in Japan wasn't red. It was yellow. But the blood they spilled from the bombs that were dropped was red like the flag. The thousands of years of defending their homes and their way of life was drenched in blood, same color as the circle of the flag. The scars they received after fighting for their lives for so long were red like blood. The red was a reminder far more than it was a tactic of war. It was a reminder not just of the good they had seen, but the bad in both themselves and others.

The Rising Sun flag reminded Burke of Lucky's scarred and haggard cheeks. It was a reminder to him of the evil in the world that tries so very hard to draw man away from goodness. That was what Lucky's scars meant to him. That was what the red circle meant to a country that woke up to a yellow rising sun.

And that was what all of John's scars meant to him. They were a reminder of the evil in the world, the anger in his mother, the fear in himself, the rage in McDuff – it was a reminder of the scars in every man. The scars reminded him that doing the good thing, the right thing, has a price. Doing the right thing was, and still is, unfortunately, extremely pricey.

NINE

Major Lowrie and Corporal Harrison gazed out from behind a line of bushes at their salvation awaiting them on the shore. It wasn't what they had hoped. Japanese forces sat along the shore of the Pacific, numbered just under one hundred in total. From their vantage point, it looked as though the soldiers were passing through, but they couldn't be sure. Regardless, Lowrie and Harrison knew that they would never make it if they stayed put much longer; the villagers would no doubt say something to the first Japanese soldier that passed through and any hope of making it off the island would have been crushed by an entire army on high alert. With their salvation so close at hand, it was time to act. On the shore sat the fishing boat of their salvation, the very one that the village boys had mentioned to Major Lowrie and Corporal Harrison. But in between them and the boat sat a hoard of enemy soldiers.

"We're screwed," Corporal Harrison buzzed quietly. "We are so screwed! How are we supposed to get there? What are we supposed to do?"

Major Lowrie peered out towards the fishing vessel, beyond the encampment of soldiers, with a look of strong determination. Corporal Harrison continued his worried jabbering until Major Lowrie eventually had heard enough. "Corporal, I need you to shut up!" he barked. Harrison retracted like an embarrassed dog. "Lieutenant Burke," Lowrie grumbled, "Come here. I think I see something."

Burke hadn't heard a word. Ever since they had escaped, all that he could seem to think about was that barren village several miles back. *It doesn't seem right,* Burke thought. *Doesn't seem right...*

"Lieutenant Burke – get over here, now!" Lowrie huffed, grabbing Burke's arm and pulling him over.

"Sorry," he replied. "What is it?"

"Look," Lowrie said, pointing to a row of trees in the jungle just beyond the Japanese shoreline camp. "You think that will be enough cover to make it through?"

John shrugged. "Sure. But there is no way around the Japanese. We move now in the daylight and they'll spot us no matter how many trees there are. As soon as we're on the water, we'll be blown away."

"We may not make it 'til then," Lowrie replied. "We may have no choice but to go now."

Corporal Harrison piped in on their conversation. "But there *is* a way to other side, right? We will make it?"

"Possibly," said Lowrie.

"We're going home!? We're going home! Ha-ha!"

"Keep your voice down, Corporal!" Lowrie hushed. "Stay focused on the plan here, soldier."

"What is the plan then?" asked Harrison.

Lowrie grew agitated. "I—I don't know. Yet."

Freedom was only a boat ride away. Burke knew that the chances of them getting picked up by an American ship were really good if they could just make it to open waters. It wouldn't even be a week until they were dropped off at a base somewhere, probably in the Solomons. Then they would be passed from base to base until they made it home to their ticker-tape hero's parade. Freedom was so very close.

Burke sat back and returned to his thoughts, leaving the other two to argue the plan among themselves. "Don't die" – it was all he could remember of home, his mother's last words to him on paper. It wasn't an invitation to come home; it was an order from an angry woman who wanted her son to come back and pay for her liquor again. It wasn't much to go home to, he thought. And that's when it struck him – fear. Deep set, unmistakable fear. He was afraid of what was waiting for him at home. A year of being locked away, not hearing a word about the war or his country or his home. Who knows what could have changed? He was afraid of what had changed, and even more afraid of what had not changed. He had no one waiting for him, no one who cared for him. He had nothing to go back to, and no one to welcome him to any kind of home.

"Lieutenant Burke," Lowrie said suddenly. "I think I've got it. We're going to get out of here!" Harrison's gaze bobbed up and he started dancing around, back and forth, in place. "We can make a pass through those trees," Lowrie explained. "If we are smart enough to start a distraction here on the north side of the shore, we can…"

"I'm staying."

Lowrie stopped. Harrison's eyes grew large. They both looked at John as though they misheard. John just sat there, wide-eyed and trembling.

"Excuse me?" Major Lowrie said slowly.

John shook his head, the fear in his eyes growing darker and darker. The words came out suddenly and caught even him by surprise.

"Did he just say what I think he did?" Harrison asked Lowrie. "Why would you say that, John? What are you – what is he talking about?"

It was in that moment that it happened. "Don't die," were the only words Burke remembered from the only person on earth left who was supposed to love him. And she was probably dead, or in a drunken coma. Then there was the zoo and McDuff… that angry, drunken tirade of a man. The bitter, breaking cold winters and stale, ugly summers. That was what he left, *on purpose.* And the sky, oh, the skies in which he flew had become nothing more than a footpath to hell. All that came down from it was fire, and death. The charred bodies of soldiers, crumbling villages, burning corpses – that was all that came out of it. And the village they had just left was next. At least, it was probably next. The whole island of Japan would be lit on fire by the time the war was over. The sky wasn't fit to fly anymore. And the black ocean with its restless bodies and…

And it was then, in that moment, that it happened. John Oscar Burke became a coward. Not of the war, but of the home he served and the skies he would have to fly. He was more afraid of those things than anything else on earth. Going back was a fate worse than death. If he didn't go back, all that was left *to* do was die, and there was one sure way of doing that.

"I'm s-staying in Japan," he uttered.

"What the hell are you talking about, soldier?" Lowrie asked angrily.

John just shrugged. "I-I can't go back there, not there. Not to fly back over this again… I'm sor—I'm not going back with you."

Lowrie reached out quickly and slapped him, then grabbed him by the shoulders. "Soldier, you are not yourself! It's been a long few months for us all, just listen to what you're saying…"

"With all due respect, Major Lowrie," Burke inserted, "I have listened to myself. Major Lowrie – Andy – I can't do it. I can't go just to go back to flying over this place and watching it burn. There's nothing back home for me and these people are…"

"These people are the enemy, soldier!"

"They are humans, Andy!"

Lowrie shoved Burke to the ground and yanked him around by the lapels. Harrison jumped back and watched Lowrie shake Burke around mercilessly. "That's Major Lowrie to you, *Lieutenant*, and what you're suggesting is called AWOL!"

"I'm done—I'm just done..." Burke whimpered.

"You get your act together, soldier!"

"Major – I'm done. Stop."

"Listen to me... you listen to me..."

"Major – I can't. I got nothing left back there. I either go back to watching more people die from the cockpit of my plane or I get beat around by my mother – if she's even still alive. I got nothing. Just let me die."

Lowrie stopped, his throat constricting around the lump that had formed there. Corporal Harrison edged closer to the men as the silence grew thick. "You're not going to let him do it, are you Major?"

Nothing was said at first.

"Major, you can't let him do it!"

Tears began to fall along the side of Burke's face. If he couldn't pull the trigger after Leo had died, then perhaps one of the Japs would do it for him. His eyes trembled at the sight of Major Lowrie hovering over him, caught off guard and without words.

"Please, let me just die here, Major..." Burke moaned again.

Suddenly, a whimper came from behind them amid the trees. The men twisted around simultaneously to look at a pair of nine-year-old eyes looking fearfully at the three men. It was Kioshi. Major Lowrie quickly sat up, releasing Burke. John climbed onto his knees and looked at the boy, whose eyes began filling with frightened tears.

"It's okay," Burke said calmly to him. "He didn't hurt me, we were just talking."

"What is he doing here?" the corporal asked nervously.

"He must have followed us from the village," Lowrie replied.

"Why is he here?" Harrison continued.

"Kioshi," asked Burke, approaching the boy slowly. "What are you doing here?"

"Do you know this kid, Burke?" Harrison inquired.

"He's just a kid I met in the village."

"Well why is he here?"

"I don't know. He must have liked us or something."

The four of them looked at each other nervously. None of them were quite sure what to do. Finally, Major Lowrie broke the silence: "He can't be here, it's too dangerous – for us and for him."

"Well, what do we do with him?" the corporal asked.

"Major – let me take him," Burke offered.

"No, you're going home.

"Let me stay – please…"

"No!"

"Sir."

Suddenly, Kioshi began to whisper and shrink back, his eyes staring up at the sky and his little hand pointing upwards. The three men took notice and slowly turned around but the hum of the engines hit their ears before they even saw them coming.

"Get down!" Major Lowrie shouted.

They all darted and ducked behind logs and trees. Seconds later, shots began reaming the beach and the coastline all around them, lead raining down past their heads and onto the soldiers on the beach. Engines ebbed and soared as they barreled and dove overhead, attacking clusters of soldiers only yards away from the four of them.

Major Lowrie stuck his head out from behind a fallen tree and waved the attention of the other men. "They're probably from a carrier!" he shouted. "It must be close, now's our chance to get to a boat!"

Corporal Harrison popped his head out from cover not far from Lowrie. "What about the kid?" he shouted back.

"Now's the time – let's move! Leave him!"

Harrison and Lowrie got up and started towards the boat. Showers of lead and shrapnel blew all around them. Behind them, towards the shore, some of the soldier's vehicles caught fire from bullets pounding into their engines. A few of the Japanese soldiers below were taking pot shots at the planes above them, ducking and running for cover along the way. The soldiers were no match; they were being torn in half by lines of bullets stripping the beach clean. Major Lowrie and Corporal Harrison took off towards the trees along the beach, away from the mayhem. Lowrie turned around mid-run and spotted Burke, who stood frozen in his place amid the cover.

"Let's go!" Lowrie shouted.

Burke paused, overwhelmed with a wave of adrenalin. He looked at Lowrie and Harrison, who stood wide-eyed and anxious. They expected him to come. They expected him to follow them and snap out of whatever it was Burke was feeling. They expected Burke to see the light and do the right thing – to go home and get the hell out of there. But there was no light for Burke to see. There was no home for Burke to go to. There was nothing but clarity for Burke, for the first time in years.

Suddenly, Burke turned and saw Kioshi, who had taken shelter behind a tree. The boy was covering his ears and was shaking miserably, covered in pee. Soon, it seemed this boy would lose everything too, Burke thought. John knew the feeling. He could not leave a child like Kioshi to die so cruelly. Assuring himself of his new resolve, Burke turned to Lowrie and Harrison. The sky over the two men was a dark, sinister blue, recovering from the brilliant yellow sun they had seen that morning. The waters below the sky had turned a dark black, as dark as night. It was the same ocean that had swallowed up Parker... and Lucky... And across the ocean was... nothing.

Behind Burke came the whimpers of a frightened, nine-year old boy, shaking and trembling uncontrollably as lead showered down and soldiers were dying all around him. John shook his head and looked back up at Major Lowrie.

"No," he said.

The major nodded. "God help you," he replied. Then he and Harrison turned and darted into the trees, heading towards the boat. And that was the last time Burke ever saw or heard of Major Lowrie and Corporal Harrison.

Kioshi let out a shrill cry. The planes were not done raking the beach clean of Japanese soldiers. As their numbers dwindled, some of the soldiers began making their way into the jungle, closer towards John and Kioshi, which meant that the fighter planes were close in tow. John quickly popped up, grabbed Kioshi in his arms, and started running like mad back towards the village. Gunfire from the fighters shot down at them through the leaves and tree branches overhead. Japanese soldiers were getting pierced with bullets not far from where they were. Kioshi cried out even louder in Burke's arms.

"Cover your eyes!" he shouted at the boy, hoping the child would hear and understand.

Burke ran a long time with Kioshi in his arms. Nearly all of the soldiers had been killed and the few that remained were still being chased and shot at by the fighters from the carrier. Burke quickly made a sharp turn away from the soldiers and bolted away from the action as best he could. The muscles in his legs were tighter than a wound-up rubber band. Kioshi's village was not far, not more than a mile away, but the weight of the child in his arms made it harder and harder for John to carry him.

Suddenly, John's foot ran up under a rock and he tripped. Kioshi sailed out of his arms and into the air. Reaching out to try and grab him, John's head led the fall and hit hard and fast on a nearby rock. He was down. The cool feeling of blood trickled down his neck from his skull. The earth around him was blurry and all he could hear were the muffled cries of little Kioshi. And that was the last thing John remembered before passing out.

PART III

ONE

Three days had passed and John was still drifting in and out of consciousness. Occasionally, he made out bright, white lights and would hear what sounded like voices humming to one another, but he could not understand anything. Eventually, ever so slowly, the words became clearer. But as they did, he found that he did not understand them any better. The Japanese nurses at the foot of his bed spoke in hushed tones to one another before noticing him stir and scurrying off. Burke could not even sit up to see the nurses' faces; the aching throb in his head caused him to lie back down as soon as he tried. It felt as though somebody had placed a lead weight in the back of his skull. The reality was that a small, metal plate had been inserted just on the outside of his skull. This fact was lost on Burke between the routine nausea, passing out, rolling over, and passing out again.

This routine continued on for days and even into weeks. As the days ambled by, it became harder and harder for John to remember what day of the week it was or even the month. The first time he really opened his eyes and took in his room was something of a rebirth.

Everything was still incredibly bright, but colors slowly began appearing. He was in a pale sort of room, lying in a bed with matching pale sheets. As he stirred, he noticed hooked to his wrist was a long tube that led to a glass canister hanging beside his bed. Burke moved to adjust the IV himself, quickly realizing he had been shackled to the bed by handcuffs. Standing outside his door, a Japanese guard stirred lazily, checking on his prisoner before returning his gaze to the boring hospital hallway.

Burke's room was brightly lit by a large window not far from his bed. Outside, a fresh snow had powdered the earth with just enough dust to cover the surface of the ash and charcoal-colored ground and the trees beneath it. John laid back and gazed dreamily at the breathtaking landscape, admiring what he could see of it before a wave of nausea suddenly overcame him. The world all around began spinning out of control, his stomach began to churn. With a sudden burst of energy, Burke shot up, leaned over the side of his bed, and upchucked onto the ground.

The guard at his post peeked inside Burke's tiny room, annoyed. "Kare ga okite iru!" he shouted to someone down the hall.

A minute later, a well-mannered nurse dressed in a starch white uniform floated into the room. She bent down and began cleaning up the vomit without making so much as an expression of disgust or annoyance. John started to thank her for her service to him, but his words fell clumsily from his mouth in inaudible mumbles. After the nurse finished cleaning the vomit, she wiped her hands clean on a rag, stood up over John's bed, and stuck out a finger in front of his eyes and began moving it around slowly. "Mito yo," she said, almost in a whisper.

John began following her finger around, up and down, and every which way. As soon as she was satisfied with his response, she quickly grabbed his wrist and took his pulse, proceeded to check his blood pressure, and swiftly scribbled something down on his chart at the foot of his bed. Then she left, not even making a sound.

For the next several hours, John didn't do much of anything. His afternoon consisted of learning to use the bedpan on his own, upchucking into the bedpan, and mumbling to another nurse as she took care of the mess quietly and respectfully. It was a dull morning for the most part and did not prove to shape into much. Suddenly, the guard at Burke's door shot up at attention as the sound of boot heels carved a path down the bland hallways. The boots stopped outside Burke's room, investigated the scene from where they were, and slowly began to make their way inside.

The men escorting the individual stayed behind as a stern-looking man, dressed in a fine pressed uniform, came in, carrying his hat underneath his arm. He had incredible posture, even when walking. The man pulled up a chair from the corner of the room and sat beside John's bed. The way he moved, with such purpose and pride, reminded Burke of the way Major Allison moved about the base at Guadalcanal. The officer looked John over from head to toe, letting out a sigh through his nose as he did. He then proceeded to look down at his own pant leg and began searching it for any remnant of lint that had snuck onto its slick, clean surface.

"Do you know who I am?" the man asked in broken English.

Burke tried to shake his head but it hurt too much to move. "No sir," he replied.

The man nodded, still searching for dust to flick off his pant leg. "My name, Lieutenant Colonel Mukai. I am commanding officer for this region." His voice was deep and grizzled. Even with a thick accent and broken English, his words demanded attention. "You are from American Army, correct?"

"Yes, sir. Air Force," John replied.

"What is your name and rank?"

"John Burke, sir. I am a lieutenant."

"Why are you here?"

Burke wanted to know the same thing. He guessed that the Lieutenant Colonel wanted to know why Burke was in Japan in general. He did not look like the kind of man who liked to be asked for clarification either. "I was shot down over Fukuoka almost a year ago, sir. The base where I was held at was attacked, people scattered, and somehow I ended up here."

Lieutenant Colonel Mukai still did not look at Burke. He kept his gaze on his own uniform. Burke began to get nervous. He figured that if the Lieutenant Colonel wanted him dead, he would have already been dead. But being kept alive didn't exactly mean mercy, either.

"You are lucky man, Lieutenant Burke. Very lucky. Do you think you are lucky man, Lieutenant Burke?" Mukai asked.

Burke wasn't sure how to answer. He began to think of all the times he had prayed for luck. At that moment, Burke wasn't sure if what he was experiencing was luck or grace. Either way, if there really was a God, he must have given Burke one or the other.

"I suppose it's grace, that I'm alive that is," Burke replied.

Mukai looked up from preening himself for just a momentary half-glance at Burke before returning to grooming himself. "Interesting answer, Lieutenant. One that I would have to agree with," he said. "Do you know how you got here?"

"No, sir."

Mukai got up and moved toward the window. He looked out at the snow fiercely, his face unyielding in the brightness of the day. "A young boy and mother brought you here. From village. They came with one of my soldier, said you save boy's life?" He turned sharply and looked down at Burke as if to confirm this. Burke lay there, motionless. "They fought for your life. Try to stop bleeding from your head. I asked them why I should help an American pig like you. But they begged, and I cannot turn my ear from my people." Mukai walked over to the side of Burke's bed and examined the top of his scalp. "Have you been told what we did?" he asked, pointing to John's head.

John strained to raise his hand up to his skull. The hair was gone. All of it. John slowly ran his fingers along the surface of his scalp until he felt the bandages covering the suture wound. The cut was fresh, and it felt as though it ran down his head forever long.

"Your head was severely damaged by the fall," Mukai continued. "We didn't think you make it. Perfect opportunity to advance our medicine. Otherwise I would not have agreed to surgery. We put a plate inside your skull to reinforce the wounded bone."

Burke started to panic. "When was this?" he asked.

"Weeks ago," Mukai replied. "We have been waiting for your recovery. You have taken long time to awaken." Mukai began to move back to his chair, putting it neatly back from where he got it. "I don't normally make exception for things of this. But I could not ignore my people. They beg for your life." Mukai came in closer to Burke, deliberately making eye contact. "I do not like Americans. I do not like you. I do not like saving your life. But whoever you are, I am obligated to owe you a debt of appreciation for saving the life of one of my people, but that is all I owe you."

Mukai started towards the door. "I will not *thank* you for what you did, even though it is worthy of thanks. Instead, I will extend to you my grace. When you recover, you will work with the others. Do not betray my grace, Lieutenant Burke. It only go so far."

John nodded. Lieutenant Colonel Mukai left the room swiftly, placing each footstep in front of the other in a determined gait. As he left, Burke laid his head back down on the pillow and stared at the ceiling. He began to wonder what had happened to Major Lowrie and Corporal Harrison. They were probably still out there, somewhere, either floating on top of the sea or somewhere in it. He hoped they were still on top of it. In a way, he wished he was there, too.

A nurse ventured in the room and began to fiddle with Burke's I.V. A shiver ran down Burke's body and he grabbed his elbows to warm himself up. The nurse took no notice. She kept fiddling with tubes and bottles and continued checking his vitals. As she did, Burke stared out the window at the snow dusting.

"What month is it?" he asked her. She looked back at him confused and, ignoring his request, kept working. "Sorry – right, no English." Burke began to pantomime day, time – anything to get his point across. Catching on, she pointed to the wall above his head. Burke attempted to turn around and look. A clock hung down low, next to a crooked Japanese calendar. The clock hands were pointed in the direction of 1:13. The calendar had been marked off up until the end.

"December?" he asked the nurse. She made no response. He figured that meant yes.

He laid his head back and stared out the window again. Light snowfall began to flake down from the sky. It was a beautiful thing to watch from his bed – it was, after all, the first bed he had slept in in almost a year.

TWO

Burke woke the next morning startled and in pain.

The I.V. tube in his arm was being yanked and pulled in several directions at once. It got his attention quickly. He twisted over in his bed to see a young, nine-year-old smiling and riding around on his I.V. pole like a rocket ship. The line from Burke's arm to the I.V. bag was taut as Kioshi pretended to be sailing around the galaxy. As he turned around the planet Saturn, his attention caught John's and he quickly stopped. Kioshi hunkered down with an apologetic glance and turned his attention sheepishly to the ground. He then quickly ran over to the foot of John's bed where his mother sat quietly.

She was a stout looking woman, with wrinkles creasing the corners of her eyes and bags drooping low underneath her eyelids. She was modestly dressed in grey clothes that hung loose around her arms. She looked as though she was in her middle to late thirties. Her arms were folded politely in her lap and her legs crossed to one side.

She looked up at John meekly, paying no attention to Kioshi, who was ducking behind her chair by then.

No one said a word at first.

"Good morning," Burke finally said, trying to break the silence.

"Ohayogozaimasu," she replied.

Burke looked to the doorway of his room. The guard posted there was standing in the doorway, watching them intently. John turned back to Kioshi's mother, who was staring at the ground, occasionally looking up at John innocently.

"Thank you for saving me," John told her. "I know you probably don't understand me, but thank you."

She smiled back at him, understanding at least the thank you.

"My name is John," he continued. "John."

She pointed to herself humbly. "Ayame."

"Ayame," Burke repeated. "Thank you, Ayame."

Kioshi tugged at his mother's sleeve and pointed to the ground. John couldn't see what it was. Ayame bent down gracefully and picked up a small package wrapped in a light paper. She gave it to Kioshi who grabbed it quickly and dashed over to the side of John's bed, handing it over excitedly.

"For me?" John asked, pointing to the package. Ayame nodded.

John took it and began unwrapping the tissue-like paper carefully, handing the paper over to Kioshi who was standing at the bedside eagerly watching him. Beneath the wrapping was a woven, thick, cloth hat. He ran his hand across and around it; its fibers were soft and gentle to the touch, soothing and warm. Ayame smiled at John again and pointed to her head, as if instructing him on how to wear it. Kioshi suddenly swiped it from John's hand and put it on his own head. It hung loose on him and waved back and forth as he bobbed around the room.

"Kioshi!" his mother scolded him.

John laughed. "Fits you well!"

Kioshi eventually took the cap off and gave it back to John with a guilty smile that only a child could muster. John took it back carefully and placed it over his own head. The site where they inserted the plate was still tender to the touch so he had to maneuver it on over his scar carefully and slowly. The cap fit snugly over his bald head, permeating warmth throughout his body. "Thank you," he told Ayame.

Kioshi tugged at John's sleeve and turned his attention to him. "Watashi o hozon shite itadaki arigatou gozaimasu," he said.

"Kare wa nihongo ga hanasenai!" his mother told Kioshi.

Kioshi ducked his head down awkwardly again and nodded. "Watashi wa mada shitte iruga," he replied. John looked at the two cluelessly and shrugged with a smile. Kioshi glanced back up at John, saying, "Oki ni arigatou."

John smiled, catching the word "arigatou." "You're welcome," he replied to the boy.

Ayame looked back at John from her chair gratefully. "Arigato," she said to him softly. He nodded in gratitude. It didn't seem right to say, "You're welcome," not after they had saved his life in return. Ayame slowly got up and motioned for Kioshi. The boy ran over to his mother and took his place beside her leg. "Dewa mata, John," his mother said.

"Goodbye," John replied. Kioshi waved at him with a toothy smile, still bobbing around excitedly.

"Kanji, Kioshi," his mother said, waving him along out the door. Kioshi darted out of the room. Ayame smiled once more at John before exiting herself. The guard at the door watched them leave and then turned and huffed at Burke before sitting back down at his post.

Burke reached up and felt the cap Ayame and Kioshi had given him. It was soft and warm, a welcome feeling for his bald head, which had grown extremely cold. Outside his window, snow drifted down from the sky gracefully. The sky had turned a grayish blue and the morning sun had turned the ground towards the east a brilliant shade of yellow. The view from the window was the best John ever had of Japan. In the distance were mountains covered in trees and brush. The valley came down low, all the way up to the hospital's doorstep, with scattered rocks and moss here and there. There wasn't a day that went by that it *wasn't* beautiful outside that window. The more John looked out, the less he regretted not going with Major Lowrie and Corporal Harrison.

From day to day, Burke didn't do much of anything but stare out his window. Life in the hospital was pretty dull, and to make matters worse, he wasn't able to stand or bend down. Most days he just lay there, staring at the beautiful picture of Japan outside his window. Somehow, for him, it didn't matter, though. Days in the hospital went by strangely quickly. It wasn't like the medical tent he was forced to endure back at Guadalcanal. It certainly wasn't as bad as the hospital he stayed in when he had his first heart attack much later in life – a place he'd later dub the "eighth level of hell." The hospital in Japan, somehow, was different. It was better.

The nurses in the hospital were the best he had ever experienced. They rarely said a word to him, checked him over quickly, and he never had to call for any of them repeatedly. There was a doctor who would come into Burke's room every once and a while to check his chart. He didn't seem much brighter to Burke than any other doctor he'd met, though. When he did come into the room, he would spend the entire time looking at Burke's charts, reviewing the things the nurses had written down or brought to him, and jabber on in medical jargon that John figured he wouldn't understand even if it was in English. The first time the doctor came in and started talking, Burke attempted to tell him that he didn't speak any Japanese. Somehow, though, John felt that even if they did speak the same language, the doctor still wouldn't have listened to a word he had to say. Apparently, John figured, not listening to the patient is a universal creed carried by doctors around the world. It must have been an oath they repeated, along with the Hippocratic oath. *I shall not listen to my patient, so help me God.* And as the doctor would go on about the chart, he would push a bunch of pills in Burke's general direction and order him to take them.

"Aka, 2 - Nichi atari," he said handing John a bottle of red pills.

"What are they?" John asked, halfway expecting an answer.

"Ao, 1 - Nichi atari," he said handing John a bunch of blue pills.

"What do those do?" John asked again. Of course, no response.

Burke never liked taking any of the meds anyways. The red ones always gave him gas and the blue ones always gave him constipation. It was the worst combination of chemicals any human could have put together, lending all the more creed to Burke's "eighth level of hell" theory. Burke eventually gave up taking the medications in lieu of stomach relief. When the doctor found that out, he started screaming at Burke in fiery Japanese and gave him a bunch of green pills that made him pass enough through his colon that he could have moved lawn furniture. This, John felt, was done out of sheer spite.

After flipping through the chart each week, the doctor would turn on his heels and whiz out of the room as quickly as he had entered. Once, one of the nurses who was tending John's bedside sneered at the doctor as he left the room. When she realized Burke had been watching, she became extremely embarrassed and dipped her head down low in shame. Burke started laughing. He found it comforting to know that he wasn't the only one who hated doctors in that country. As the nurse realized that it was okay to make fun of her boss, she started giggling too. For the moment, Burke and the nurse bonded deeply. They might not have spoken the same language, but they at least shared a common enemy.

The staff in the hospital fed him, kept him stable, managed his pain – did all the things medical professionals should do but, in Burke's life, largely hadn't. After a few more days of recovery, a nurse started coming in with a guard to unhook him from his bed so he could walk around a bit. The guard never liked this part of his job, probably feeling a sense of waste in his "war efforts," which Burke always felt somewhat guilty for. By the end of the month, Burke was walking by himself and moving around on his own. Things at first were a bit slow, but he progressed all right. Eventually, hair even started to grow back around his head except on the top of his scalp where the plate was.

Towards the end of his stay in the hospital, Burke was able to walk all the way down the hall by himself and back without stopping. It felt at first as though he was hiking Mount Kilimanjaro, but the task got easier and easier. Burke later remembered walking down the hallway, past the rooms of the other patients. He noticed quickly that all of the other patients in the hospital were Japanese soldiers. Nobody in the hospital looked like they were in good shape, either. A lot of the men had lost limbs; some of them didn't look like they were ever going to wake up. New patients were being rolled in almost daily. Nurses would whizz a soldier down the hall on a stretcher followed by a doctor in tow who was frantically rattling things off from the patient's chart while nobody paid attention. Usually, the patient would be bleeding profusely and somebody would be trying to stop the bleeding as best they could. Even with all that was going on, though, it was rarely loud. Everybody in the hospital moved to their places quietly but determined. There was no yelling or screaming and rarely did the patients holler or yell. The only time Burke ever heard a peep out of any of them, really, was because they were experiencing some kind of excruciating pain. The quiet was reverent and serious. It was as if everyone in the hospital, from patients to doctors, knew the seriousness that the field of medicine held. They all respected it and didn't yell or scream or get in the way of it. They just let it happen, got it over with, and respected the hell out of it. John never understood why this wasn't so in America.

One day, as Burke was walking down the hallway guided by one of the guards, he walked past a room of a soldier who was dying. Inside the room, the family members lined the bedside of the solider. He did not move, did not open his eyes. He was a younger looking man, a little older than Burke, but the life in his body had looked as though it had already gone. None of the family members said a word and nobody cried. John watched as one of the older women – what looked to be a grandmother or great aunt – moved towards the soldier's bedside and began washing his face with a wet cloth. Another woman began to wash the young soldier's hands. One of the men in the room then spoke softly, gesturing towards the young soldier as the others paid their respects with an incredible integrity. The guard accompanying Burke down the hall stopped and looked in the doorway, paying a respectful glance at the young soldier. One of the children in the room crossed over to the soldier and placed a dagger in the his hands. An adult who had ushered the child over crossed the soldier's arms across his chest with the dagger firmly in his hand.

The guard escorting Burke finished paying his respects to the soldier and turned to Burke. He huffed and motioned for them to keep moving down the hallway. John nodded and started back down the pale corridor. As he left the doorway of the dead soldier, John offered the family one last glance of sympathy. Even the children, he noticed, had an honest and sincere fear of what was happening. It was an incredibly touching sight to see. It made John think of Leo and how he had sent his friend off to the other side, alone. Neither this Japanese family nor John enjoyed the process in the least. They all had a fear of it – dying. And yet, they all had been responsible for the other's death. As they buried their dead, John figured they all knew that it was senseless for their death to occur, an act of violence towards one another that never needed to get this out of hand. There was no point placing blame. Both sides contributed their share. It was just how it was.

Awarding blame, John eventually concluded, was neither here nor there. This family's son/brother/father died right in front of all of them, and the respect they paid their dearly beloved somehow made Burke feel better about leaving Leo out in the jungle all alone. While they may not have respected Americans in the war, Burke realized that the Japanese sure as hell respected the dead, like all real humans would. Somewhere, out in the jungle outside Fukuoka, Leo got his proper burial, the one he deserved, by people who honestly respected him in death.

That night, in the hospital, Burke slept better than he had in months.

It was January of 1945 when Burke finally left the hospital. The war was still raging on and John had already been shot down, captured by the enemy, and been the subject of medical experimentation by people he had never met before. Truth was, being stuck in Japan through 1945 was the best thing that had happened to him during the war. Granted, Burke was a coward, afraid of going back home or of being forced to destroy more human lives from across the ocean. And granted, Burke had technically gone AWOL when he decided to not go along with Major Lowrie and Corporal Harrison. But for Burke, as January of 1945 rolled around, he was okay with being a wartime coward. He thought of Kioshi and Ayame and the poor village where he had first met the boy, and realized something that truly changed him – over the ocean, there was the fear of more death to come. But in Japan, in the hearts of a nine-year-old boy and his mother, there was hope and a little bit of grace.

THREE

Close to three months ambled by. The time had mostly consisted of Burke scrubbing floors and picking up animal (and human) dung. For Burke, it felt like a throwback to his time at McDuff's zoo, only with less alcohol and screaming. His hair had still not quite grown back by then either. It was still very cold in Japan in March, but it was nothing as cruel as January or February had been. Though without the cap he had received from Ayame and Kioshi, his head would have frozen solid. He could almost feel the plate in his head begin to freeze separately from the rest of his scalp at times. In fact, it took him nearly a year to adjust to the metal plate in his head before it became somewhat unnoticeable.

There were really no other Americans in the area. The ones who were there were usually dead or dying soldiers gathered up from having been shot out of the sky. It was rare that a pilot was shot down, but when they were, it wasn't pretty. Needless to say, Burke began to grow quieter and quieter in the absence of anyone to talk to.

As for English-speaking Japanese, there were virtually none to speak of. A few of the educated kids would come near the base from time to time. They knew a little English that they had learned in school, but the extent of it usually ranged from "how are you," to "my favorite color is blue, what is yours?" Outside of this, Burke and the kids had nothing more to really talk about. The kids, in the excitement of learning a new language, would still flock to John to test out their new English skills. They usually just ended up telling each other what their favorite and least favorite colors were. Before long, many of the kids began to refer to Burke as the "Aka" man, which he found out translated to "red" man, as he repeatedly told them his favorite color was red. This always brought a smile to Burke, and when the kids would ask him why it was funny, he would try to explain to them what "red man" really meant in America. Nevertheless, the racial slur usually ended up lost in translation for the kids.

March wasn't a fun time for Japan. It wasn't fun for any of the people on the island, John included. Things in the Pacific were getting rougher and the fighting was closing in on the mainland faster and faster. By that time, American forces had finally taken the island of Iwo Jima a couple hundred miles off the coast of Japan after months of fighting. Where John was being held, on the shores near Nobeoka about 80 miles south of Hiroshima, the Japanese army had to sit and listen to their brothers in arms die alone on the banks of Iwo Jima without the ability to do anything about it. About six thousand American forces were killed in the fighting; a whopping twenty-one thousand Japanese forces were killed. Considering there were only twenty-two thousand men stationed on the island in the first place, it was an understatement to say that Iwo Jima was a total loss for the Japanese.

Burke's job, most days, was to clean the filth and grime off of anything that accumulated filth and grime in the camp. Lieutenant Colonel Mukai had kept him alive as a favor to the people of the village where Kioshi and Ayame lived. In honesty, Mukai had no real idea of what to do with John once he came out of the hospital. He put him to work scrubbing floors and emptying the toilets in exchange for his life and a few scraps of leftover food. At first, there wasn't much food available to set aside for him, but as soldiers began to disappear from the camp, food began to become less sparse. Burke could tell things were getting worse for Japan the more he was able to eat. It wasn't a glamorous job, cleaning out human waste from toilets, but it kept him alive and under the grace of the Lieutenant Colonel, so he did so without complaining.

For the first few months he was there, John rarely ever saw Lieutenant Colonel Mukai. He was okay with this. He knew it would have been a disgrace for Mukai to be seen talking to him anyways. Nearly every morning Mukai would make it a point to stand on the shores of Nobeoka and look out at the rising sun coming up over the vast horizon. Burke, who rarely slept a great deal anyways, often watched Mukai do this every day. The further along the fighting in Iwo Jima got, the more sunken Mukai's eyes became and the longer he stood on the beach after the sun had risen. All of the men at the base in Nobeoka felt the loss of Iwo Jima and it shook them to their core to watch its beaches fill with the blood of their friends and family. It catapulted them to fight harder, but it also made them writhe in pain as well.

The village where Kioshi and Ayame lived was about five miles to the north of the base near Nobeoka. Typically, every weekend or so, Ayame and Kioshi would come down to the base to see how John was doing. The guards always kept their eyes turned sharply on them when they visited. John had his own room, about the size of a closet, where he lived and he was only allowed to come out to work or to eat. So, in order for Ayame and Kioshi to see him, they had to bring him food of some sort so that they could eat and see him at the same time. This was a regular occurrence for several weeks, up through the end of March 1945. The three didn't have much to talk about, mostly due to the language barriers, but John took comfort in the thought that someone in the world cared for his life in some honest and real way.

The last time the three of them ate together on the beaches of Nobeoka was the last weekend of March, the same week Iwo Jima fell. Ayame and Kioshi had brought him fish; it was a considerate and thoughtful gift, but Burke never had the guts to tell them how much he hated raw fish. Considering their gratitude, however, and his constant hunger, he never raised a fuss. During the week since Ayame and Kioshi's last visit, John had collected a few twigs and bamboo shavings that he had tied together in his spare time to make a figurine for Kioshi. It was a silly looking thing, with all the quality and craftsmanship of a preschool arts and crafts project. But, when he gave it to Kioshi, the boy thought it was the greatest thing in the world, his face lighting up with new life when he saw it.

The bamboo shavings stuck out in all places and the arms of the little man were crooked, one considerably longer than the other. Kioshi twirled it around in his hands and looked at Burke curiously for an explanation. John thought of the best excuse he could come up with for his poor craftsmanship.

"It's an Indian toy, like from America," he told him. Kioshi was still unsure. "American toy," John said louder, foolishly thinking that increased volume would break the language barrier. Still nothing. John, conceding to his poor communication skills, made an "O" with his mouth and patted it with his hands like the Indians in the Western movies did. "Red man, Aka man," he told him.

Kioshi smiled and pointed to John. "Aka man!" he shouted, smiling from ear to ear.

"No, no it's not me," he replied. Of course, it was too late. Kioshi had already bought into the explanation that John was the stick man and he wasn't going to take any other explanation.

"Aka man! Aka man!" he shouted, showing his mother. She smiled at her son and patted his head.

"Arigato," she said to John.

"You're welcome," he replied graciously.

Ayame and Kioshi's visits were by far the best part of John's week. If, for some reason, they didn't show up during the weekend, the following week felt twice as long. They never could say much, despite John's poor attempt at learning basic words, but for some reason that was all okay. The last week they were on Nobeoka together was a great time for the three of them. Eventually, as was custom, the guard came by and broke up their communion together, pushing Burke back to his locked closet.

"I'll see you around," he told Ayame and Kioshi as he was leaving. The kiddo grinned a massive grin as only a child could, waving wildly. Ayame, for the first time, looked at John in the eyes as he was leaving, placed her hand over her heart, and bowed her head. He had never seen her or anyone else do it before. The guard escorting John back sneered to Ayame and yanked Burke harder towards his room.

The next day, things around the base began quietly. As it was, Ayame and Kioshi had stayed the night near the base and were preparing to leave while Burke was doing his morning duties. Then it happened.

As he was hauling another load of waste to the dump, Burke stopped and looked over at Ayame and her son, who were packing their things to go. The two looked back tenderly at him, smiling and giving one last wave before leaving. Suddenly, the familiar rumble they had all grown to fear rolled in from the clouds over the black waters.

The first wave came suddenly and without introduction.

Firebombs exploded all around. Flames burst behind them along the coast, fires raging all around, and men shot madly at the sky. John ran over to Ayame and Kioshi and grabbed them under their arms. He took them into the jungle to a small nook underneath some rocks. Kioshi was crying like mad and Ayame was covering her ears, trembling more with each blast. Burke sprawled out over them with his body.

"It's going to be okay," he whispered in their ears. "Hang on… It will pass."

Ayame was whispering to herself something of a prayer. She quaked with fear, from her fingers to toes, as she clung to her son, in fear for his life. Kioshi was underneath them both. In his little hands, he held tightly the Aka man close to his chest.

"Make this stop," John whispered to God. "Enough already. Enough!"

Suddenly, the bombs stopped falling. The planes above them soared overheard and made their flip, returning home. The roar of the flames on the beach cracked and moaned as buildings and structures crumbled to the ground. John turned his head around and assessed the damage. It wasn't as bad as the damage on Mount Sefuri, but there were dozens of dead bodies strewn across the beach. The stench of burning flesh quickly caught their noses. Kioshi let out a wail.

"It's going to be okay," Burke whispered in his ear. He touched Ayame's shoulder and she shot up with a jolt. Tears had soaked the sides of her cheek and she was still trembling all over.

"Stay here," John instructed her, putting his palm up to stop her from getting up. "I will come back." He wanted to see how bad the damage was from the other side and see if he could help. The need to do something burned madly within him. Ayame tugged at his arm to try and get him to stay. "I'll be back," he said, brushing her off and running to the beach. "I promise I won't leave you!"

Flames were everywhere on the beach and men were frantically trying to put out fires all around the base. Over the waters, American bombers made their way back to wherever they had come from, safe and sound. Burke couldn't help but think that that could have been him. If he had not been shot at, starved, beaten, and humiliated as a prisoner in Japan, it could have been *him* delivering the bombs and headed home safe and sound. As he thought about it, he became overwhelmed with guilt and fear.

John fell to his knees, buckling under the weight of the destruction and death all around him. "If you can hear me," he prayed, "and you give a *rat's ass* about me, oh God, help my soul... Please... forgive my soul for what I've done to these people already... if you can... Oh, God..."

On the beach, edging up alongside him, Lieutenant Colonel Mukai approached in a defeated and embarrassed limp. His face was bloodied and the right side of his body had been crushed and mangled. Burke stayed on his knees and dared not get up, dared not even look him in the eye. Mukai stood there, hovering over John for a good five, nearly ten minutes. His great, confident stature began to collapse and his dignity melted into the sand underneath his feet. Finally, without looking down at Burke, Mukai said, "Are the woman and boy still here?"

"Y-yes, sir," Burke replied.

Mukai looked down at him slowly. His face was even more bruised and a vein had burst in one eye, turning it blood red. "Take them back," he said to John, staring him straight in the eye. "Send them to Hiroshima; get them away from here. Protect them," he ordered.

Burke nodded. "Yes, sir," he replied. He knew he owed it to Mukai to protect them after Burke had spent the first part of the war trying to kill them. It was the only thing he could do to regain some honor.

Mukai looked straight ahead and made his way slowly to the water. Behind him, the base had been mangled and destroyed. His soldiers were burning and their bodies were decomposing in the flames. The war had no longer become a point of who was right or even of retaliation. Both sides had lost meaning. It had become meaningless.

John ran back to Ayame and Kioshi. They were right where he had left them, still trembling wide-eyed as he approached. "Come on, let's go," he said, waving them over to him. They came without hesitation and the three began to make their way north towards the village. Ayame and Kioshi followed close in tow behind Burke, never veering too far from him. They moved quickly through the jungle. By twilight, they had made it to the village.

Upon their arrival, the other women of the village flocked out of their homes in grateful praise of Ayame and Kioshi making it back safely. The flames from the base behind them lapped up into the air wildly and smoke plumes covered the sky to the south. The women of the village ushered the three of them into one of the huts and gave them all soup and blankets. Ayame began to speak frantically, though softly, to the other ladies, occasionally pointing to John. The women stopped as she did and they all looked at him simultaneously. When Ayame had finished her story, there was complete silence in the room with all eyes on Burke. One of the women finally said something to him in Japanese and bowed her head reverently. The others followed in suit. Then, they turned their conversation inward and started chatting amongst themselves.

In the corner, by a small fire one of the women had lit, Kioshi sat balled up, clutching his red man figurine tightly. Burke wandered over and crouched down next to him. Kioshi, without looking at Burke, seemed to like this. Burke patted his head and positioned himself so that the boy could lean up against him and fall asleep.

"I'm sorry for all this, kiddo," John said to Kioshi as the boy lay there, trying his best to fall asleep. "I'm really very sorry."

Ayame eventually came over and joined the boys, sitting across the fire from them. She looked haggard and worn, but still considerably better than earlier. She leaned towards John and, dipping her head down, said, "Ka go, John. Ten on."

"Thank you," John replied, unsure of the translation. He knew what "Ten on," meant. It had something to do with God's grace. From what he could tell, she was saying something like, "God keep you, in grace."

At the time, Burke was still not sure what to think of God. In some ways, God seemed like a cruel puppeteer, orchestrating or exacting some form of cruel punishment on them all. Other times, Burke knew that it was clear that there was something other than his pitiful efforts keeping him alive. For what purpose, he wasn't sure. And what's more, he wasn't sure if it was grace or luck that was doing it for him either. If it was grace, he wasn't sure he really deserved it, not after the insurmountable debt he owed to the families of those he killed. He realized that as he watched the planes attack Nobeoka and depart; deep down he was feeling shame. In some ways, he felt that it would have been better for the world if he had simply shot himself when he first landed in Japan. He felt he deserved it, anyway.

Yet, as a gentle, nine-year-old boy fell asleep, at peace in John's lap, he no longer felt like the coward. John could not imagine what more both sides could do to the other that had not already been done. By the end of March 1945, John had seen it all: death, sorrow, anguish, abuse, and shame. What was left to see?

Unbeknownst to him at the time, there was one thing that he could never have imagined happening. He would soon see it with his own eyes, as he did the rising sun. One new thing under the sun still remained to be seen, and it would change everything.

FOUR

Every time Burke saw a flag displayed on a pole up in the air, he saw it differently than a flag put behind glass and mounted on a wall. In some respects, Burke wished that he could have displayed his Japanese flag on a pole instead of on his wall. He never could have, though, and he wouldn't have really done it even if he could. For one, he knew that if people saw him raising a Japanese flag up underneath an American one, especially right after the war, he would have been spit on, yelled at, and run out of town, if not thrown in jail for some inane reason. Second, his Japanese flag meant more than an ordinary Japanese flag. It deserved to be respected only in the most reverent of ways. But regardless, for a flag to fly high on a pole way up in the air, it automatically takes on a meaning beyond that of a flag displayed behind glass.

A flag that is mounted on the wall is seen from only one side. You see that country's flag by that one side and you miss all the other angles of viewing it. The flag doesn't get to show off its colors by flapping in the wind or by hanging down loosely on a calm afternoon. When on the wall, it is ironed out flat atop matting and hung as if it were in a gallery or museum. When it is hung like this, the flag is almost meant to serve as a symbol or reminder of what *had* happened to that country *years* ago. But when it is hung from a pole, seen from all angles, the flag is not something just to be looked at. It becomes alive. It sways and moves, dodges and ducks, gets shot at and weathered just like the people of its country have. As a veteran much later in his life, John would see an American flag brought in on a pole and would remember not just the stuff that *had* happened *years* in the distant past. He would see a living, breathing, moving thing that had suffered and weathered the same storms he had. That meant a lot to him. The American flag flew over his head for years as he was shot at and it had watched the same things he had watched throughout the war and beyond. And while the veterans died and passed away, the flag always remembered what those veterans saw.

The flag lives to tell other generations what injustice in the world looks like.

However, for nearly two years of Burke's life, the American flag could not fly over his head, see what he saw, or go where he went. For almost two years the Japanese flag took its place as it watched what he watched from the beaches and mountains of Japan. In truth, that is why Burke secretly held a love/hate relationship with the Japanese flag that hung in his home after the war. He hated it, because together they both saw some of the most chaotic, violent moments together. It reminded him of those moments. They both had seen the worst, and they both hated it. But he knew for as long as he lived that even after he died, the flag would carry the story of the two years he had spent away from the American flag. The Japanese flag that hung in his dining room told the story that he never could tell.

It was early April, 1945. The bombing of the beach near Nobeoka had been less than a week prior. John remembered watching two Japanese flags wave in the wind on the horizon, attached to a couple of Japanese military jeeps approaching the village. The flags, as well as the few men who came back with them, had survived only barely and had managed to carry themselves to the village in disarray. In the two days in between the bombing of Nobeoka and the military jeeps' arrival, Burke had managed to communicate to the villagers that they would all be much safer if they moved towards Hiroshima. Even with the language barrier, the people listened and agreed. Hiroshima was nearly two hundred miles from the village. The trip would have easily taken a week for everybody to make; vehicles were sparse and the villagers who remained were in bad shape. Before the jeeps arrived, they had taken time to collect food and a few essential belongings in order to prepare for the trip. John had planned to get the people moving towards Hiroshima the day the military jeeps had arrived. In the lead vehicle sat a defeated, but determined, Lieutenant Colonel Mukai.

As the jeeps approached, John, who had been helping Ayame and Kioshi pack for the trip to Hiroshima, dropped what he was doing and approached the vehicles cautiously as they neared. Mukai stepped out while the vehicle was still coming to a stop and marched towards him. "What are they still doing here!?" he shouted.

"We are preparing to go," John replied. "We needed time. The people will be ready to leave for Hiroshima by tomorrow."

Mukai clapped his hands at Ayame and few of the other villagers nearby who were moving food into their homes. "Isoide!" he shouted. "We need to go from here. Come with me," he grunted at Burke, waving him towards the jeeps.

"Wait, where are we going? I thought you wanted me to travel with the people to Hiroshima?" John asked.

"I told you to move people away from here, not go with them," he shot back.

John looked over at Ayame who was looking back at him for some sort of interpretation. "But what about the people? How will they make it to--"

"My people know their way around own country," said Mukai. "They do not need American filth to take them. Your debt belong to me, no debt to them. I give you grace, not them. Come!"

Burke slowly followed Mukai towards the jeep. Ayame followed in tow. "Anata wa doko e iku no ka!?" she asked Mukai.

"Modoru! Kare wa watashi no monodesu!" he replied.

"How will the people get to Hiroshima safely?" Burke asked.

Mukai spun around and glared at Burke fiercely. "No questions. My men will take people to Hiroshima, you do not go. They will be safe there. You stay here and work on planes for us."

"You *want* to stay in Nobeoka? You're exposed now, there is no protection on the coast." John replied.

"Quiet!"

Mukai's face burned with offense. Burke shut up quickly. Ayame continued to follow the men, begging Mukai. As she reached out to touch his arm, Mukai quickly shrugged her off while several soldiers accompanying him kept her back. John turned around to her, feeling as forlorn and scared as she was. "I'm sorry," he said to her quietly.

Suddenly, Ayame stood tall and shouted, "Watashi mo taiszai shimasu!"

Mukai spun back around and pointed at her directly. "Ta no hito to issho ni iku!"

Ayame shook her head and stood her ground. His face turning bright red, Mukai clenched down in anger.

"What did she say?" Burke asked him.

"She want to stay."

"Why?" Burke asked.

"She want to thank you for saving son."

"No," Burke said, turning to her. "No, no, Ayame, you must go! Keep Kioshi safe, please."

"Watashi mo taiszai shimasu," she said again, desperately. They all stood there, each waiting for the other to back down.

"If she want to die here for you, she may," Mukai said suddenly dragging Burke into the jeep.

"Ayame, don't stay," John warned her.

"Watashi wa todomaru," she replied. Burke grew agitated, frustrated that he could not beg her to stay in her own language; she remained steadfast in her resolve. Suddenly, Kioshi appeared out from a village hut behind them. He was crying loudly as he watched the soldiers drag Burke and sit him down in a jeep. "Daijobu," Ayame said, getting down and embracing the boy.

"The boy goes! Shonen wa ikanakereba naranai!" Mukai shouted.

Kioshi cried harder. His mother whispered calmly in his ear and hugged him tightly. An older woman, who looked to be Kioshi's grandmother, came and started to pull the child away, back to the village to be with the others.

"It's okay," Burke shouted to Kioshi, "It's going to be okay! Just go." Kioshi let out another cry and pushed the older woman away. He broke through the guard's legs and ran over the side of the jeep. Burke got down and grabbed the boy before he could crawl in. Mukai shouted something again in Japanese, growing angrier and more impatient. "It will be okay," John reassured the boy. Kioshi looked back at him with tears in his eyes, snot trickling down his upper lip. He was a sight. Burke patted his head and continued to reassure the boy, trying to push him back to the older woman who opened her arms to him eagerly.

"Go," Burke told him. "Ike."

Kioshi then lifted his red man toy that Burke had crafted him, as if wanting to give it to Burke as a good luck charm.

"It's yours. You keep it. It will keep you safe," said Burke.

Kioshi nodded and then wrapped his arms around Burke's neck. John hugged him back, praying to God that the child would be okay. Without delay, a soldier swept up from behind them, grabbed Kioshi, and dragged him to the older woman who promptly took him and started back to the village with the others. As quickly as she could, Ayame ran over and embraced her son again, whispering blessings in his ear before running over to the jeeps and getting in herself. John could tell from the boy's reaction that she told him she would come for him soon.

Mukai motioned for the driver to get the jeep going. The other jeep remained at the village as the rest of the soldiers prepared the people to leave. In silence, the four – Burke, Ayame, Mukai, and the driver – drove back towards the shore. For as long as she could, Ayame kept her eyes on the village and her son. She did the best she could to keep the tears from falling down her tired and worried cheeks.

"They will be safe," Mukai said to Burke, keeping his gaze on the road ahead. "Whatever it was you do for her, she pays you back with her life now," he continued, motioning to Ayame.

Burke looked at her, even though she did not look back as she was still affixed on the village. She offered her life to him, not out of obligation, but out of love. He sat amazed.

"We need to prepare planes for counterattack against Americans for when they return," Mukai informed Burke.

"You think they are coming back this direction?" he replied.

"They will return!" Mukai shot back. "We must protect people here. Many men died in bombing. I need you to work on planes to get them ready for counterattack. You work on planes, correct?"

"I know some things about working on them, yes."

"Good," Mukai grumbled. His request to Burke seemed to make Mukai nauseous, but everyone in the jeep knew how desperate Mukai was. He needed the man power, even if it required unclean hands to help.

They broke through the jungle onto the beach where what remained of the base sat still burning in heaps of ashes. Several temporary structures were put up in place of them and a couple of the buildings appeared to have been salvaged from the rubble. As they pulled up through the camp, Burke could see mounds of bodies towards the rear of the camp. They were being burned, as one great heap. No time for individual reverence. No time to remember. The few who remained on their feet looked wiped, tired, and worn, however steadfast. Eventually, the jeep passed through the camp onto a small runway where a few remaining planes were stationed. It had been severely damaged, but there were already several dozen men working on it, getting it ready to be used again. The planes that remained all appeared in terrible shape and in need of a great amount of work.

"I give you supplies and you fix," Mukai snapped at Burke.

"Oka… Yes, sir," Burke replied. Mukai said nothing in return.

John could hear the cries that escaped from Ayame's clenched face as she bore down hard on her seat. She was transfixed on the floorboards, trying hard to hold herself together. No doubt she was thinking about her son, wondering if she had made the right decision – to offer her life to the man who saved her son's life, twice. Burke wondered the same thing. Why was she doing it?

"She is indebted to you, as you are to me," Mukai said to Burke, noticing his worry. Burke turned to him, surprised he said anything. "You save her life twice – she owes you same." John nodded his head and looked back to Ayame. He wished as hard as he could to release her of coming back and just send her with Kioshi. It was suicide. It would not be long before the Americans came back and took out what was left of Nobeoka, especially if Mukai got his planes off the ground. Burke didn't want Ayame to give him her life; he just wanted her to be safe. Yet Burke realized they were all indebted to something. Ayame was indebted to him; he was indebted to Mukai; Mukai was indebted to Japan. They each owed the other everything for saving their lives.

Once they arrived, they did not waste a moment in getting the planes ready. They quickly hit the ground and began working on the planes, runway, and defense systems. Burke poured his sweat into each of the planes for weeks, getting them ready to go. Ayame found herself breaking her back over the airstrip as well. Above them, the skies stayed clear and blue, but all around them they could hear the rumble of engines tearing down encampments to the north and south. With each bomb that exploded in the distance, they worked harder than the day before, frantically putting up what defenses they had to protect the innocent villagers in the area. They rarely took a day off and when they did, it was because they were waiting for a shipment of supplies to come in so that they could get back to work on the planes.

Ayame spent most of her time making food for the soldiers, constantly fetching water throughout the day to make sure they did not dehydrate. It was taxing, but she never complained. None of them complained. They all knew the debt they owed to the other for offering each other their lives in total service. They all knew the debt they owed underneath the Japanese flag, which saw the same blood and destruction they had all witnessed.

They worked in desperation all throughout that summer. Two long and excruciating weeks after starting on repairs, the workers caught word that the villagers made it to Hiroshima safely. Leading up to that message, Burke hardly slept and Ayame slept fewer hours still. For the weeks that followed the villager's announcement, though, the workers were able to keep some communication with Hiroshima and relay information back. They were only able to correspond with each other once every week and a half or so, but it was enough to help them all sleep through the night, at least once anyways.

May passed by quickly and quietly for Nobeoka, but by the end of June 1945, things quickly grew worse. To the east, Osaka had been bombed to the ground. Word came in sporadically that Japanese forces on the other side of Japan had begun retreating back as far as China. American forces had made it on the ground all the way to Okinawa, a prefecture only a couple hundred miles off the southern shores of Japan. Even the Australians had managed to take Brunei, Borneo in only three days' time. In Kyushi, southern Japan, airfields like the one in Nobeoka were being demolished by air raids in attempts to make sure there could be no retaliation in the air from Japanese on Allied forces. Worst of all, word came through that Admiral Ota Minoru, commander in the southern Japanese waters, committed ritualistic suicide after failing to defend Okinawa. The loss shook everyone on base, even Burke although he wasn't quite sure why. It was, perhaps, the prevailing sense that things were coming to a head quickly and Burke felt that he was right in the midst of the thick. As word of these events came trickling in, the men on the small airfield in Nobeoka grew quieter and quieter. Their brothers and fathers in the north and the south were dying and giving up the fight slowly but surely.

July suddenly turned what fears they had into full-blown terror. Word made it to Noboeka that General MacArther in America had announced that the Phillippines had been liberated of Japanese forces completely. Furthermore, Norway and Italy (defecting from the Axis powers) also decided to join the fight in the Pacific and declared war on Japan. The Japanese began to feel heat in every direction. Tokyo, having been firebombed for weeks already, had begun receiving attacks from the U.S. Navy as well. The Allied leaders began demanding the unconditional surrender of Japan, who in turn refused to budge. Cities were being totaled, battleships were being sunk, and lives were still being lost. Japan still remained silent. If anything, the men on the base in Nobeoka grew quieter in terror of possible defeat, but they also grew more steadfast in their resolve.

It was finally the end of July. The airfield in Noboeka was functional and most of the planes were ready to go. Word came through from the north that airfields, like theirs, in Kobe and Nagoya were being specifically targeted, destroyed, and totaled by relentless bombings. Eventually, as enough word came in, Lieutenant Colonel Mukai brought Ayame in and told her to go. The way things were going for them, it was best for her to leave for Hiroshima as well. If Kobe and Nagoya were being totaled so quickly, it would be no great surprise when Noboeka would be destroyed as well. Mukai gave her three days to get prepared to leave with a convoy of men to Hiroshima. Their departure date was August 1, 1945.

Word was sent to the villagers in Hiroshima that Ayame was coming and to expect her soon. On August 1, Ayame and the soldiers going with her packed their things and began on their way. Burke did not know what to say exactly. As they said goodbye, the two stood across from each other, merely taking in the other's presence. Burke felt peace, but he did not know why. To the ground fell a tear from Ayame's cheek; it fell from a half-formed smile. She bowed, ever so slightly to him, glanced into his eyes tenderly, and turned to go, overflowing with grace. She was off to Hiroshima, to be reunited with her son. It was August 2, 1945.

As the vehicles started on their way, one of the soldiers excitedly waved them down and pointed to the ground beneath them. The vehicle stopped. Behind them, an engine leak in the main line trailed oil along the beach. Angrily, they all stepped out of the vehicle and assessed the situation. Ayame looked nervously at the men, hoping one of them would have a way to reunite her with her son that day. Nobody had a solution and even Burke grew frustrated quickly. He ached for Ayame who would have to wait even longer to see her son, whom she had not seen in weeks.

One of the men pointed to the other jeep at the camp. Mukai shook his head and grunted. He no doubt wanted to keep the other jeep on hand in case they needed it for an emergency and to him this was no emergency. They would have to order parts and fix the jeep before going to Hiroshima, and that was exactly what they did.

It took the parts several days before arriving at Nobeoka. During that time, Ayame busied herself with trivial work aimlessly trying to preoccupy her brain with something other than not getting to see Kioshi. No doubt the people in Hiroshima were growing nervous of Ayame's absence and this wore on her even more. Burke watched her with nervous anticipation, hoping the materials would arrive quickly. Finally, on August 5, 1945, the parts arrived for the jeep. Immediately the men began working on the vehicle, much to the nervous excitement of Ayame and her not-so-gentle prodding to get the job done quickly. Word was sent to Hiroshima to expect Ayame and the other soldiers the following day. Ayame and her son would finally be reunited; this, in turn, made Burke feel much better about the whole situation.

Of course, it wasn't going to be the last time Burke saw Ayame. In fact, she never made it out of Nobeoka on August 6, 1945. On that day, before they left for Hiroshima, something that had never happened under the Rising Sun, or anywhere for that matter, happened and it happened right in the middle of Hiroshima. And when Burke and Ayame and the others saw it happen from the beaches of Nobeoka, their very souls were crushed under the immense weight of its terrible smoke and fire. A silence would roll over the land afterwards that Burke had never experienced before or ever again in all his life.

That day, August 6, 1945, was the day that the Japanese flag stopped flying so high and stopped waving so tall up on the poles. It doubled over, instead, and reeled around madly in pain. That was the day that every Japanese flag wretched in pain because underneath them, on the ground, would come destruction like the world had never seen.

FIVE

Through the haze and fog of the morning, nothing made a sound. Dead silence. An eerie grey covered the land and visibility, especially over the dark ocean, was partial at best. Nothing flew in the sky and nothing in its right mind would have, Burke thought. In fact it was the first thought he had when we woke up and looked out over the ocean, his toes digging themselves deep within the sand. The skies were empty, and to fly in such weather would be insane.

Suddenly, there was a flash, brighter than the sun itself. The earth and sand beneath Burke's toes began to rumble and quake uncontrollably. He twisted around quickly. In the north, a bowl of bright, illuminated smoke bellowed up from the earth.

Everyone on the beach stopped dead still.

The sound of thunder came rolling towards them. It got louder. And louder. It became unbearable. The sound shrieked past their ears and out towards the ocean in a mad, rushing wind. Every tree and shrub on the ground bent back, trying hard to get away from the blast waves. A cloud rose above the city bigger and greater than anything God's hands had made. The cloud was so tall it began to fold in on itself at the top and turned mushroom-shaped underneath the darkness of the grey skies above.

No one spoke.

Suddenly, Ayame, who was standing but a few feet away from John, hurdled over in a terrifying screech. She wretched over in agony, thrashing around on the ground violently. Lieutenant Colonel Mukai took two steps toward the plume of smoke and fell to his knees before it. All across Japan, men and women reeled back and cried, aching in a pain that no one on earth had ever felt before. The last new thing under the sun had been dropped on Hiroshima, and the whole earth shook from it.

Burke had never before in his life seen something like it. And he did not just see it once. He saw it twice. Three days later, to the southwest, Nagasaki lit up with the same wave of destruction that they had seen Hiroshima erupt in. Japan had been reduced to rubble in the north and turned to ash in the south. In the middle of Hirsoshima and Nagasaki, Burke helplessly sat watching the earth crumble beneath his feet. He never could put real words to describe what he felt on those days. Ash reigned down from the blackened sky, the earth all over turned stale and gray, and smoke covered every inch of the country and lingered for days.

August 10, 1945: John weakly hunkered down on the beaches of Nobeoka, looking out over the ocean that was lapping up at his feet. All of the land was silent. Everything seemed to grow darker and darker. Within the void of the waters, good men – both Japanese and American – died lonely deaths in the blood and ash-soaked waves.

John wept for hours.

He punched the earth beneath him, cursing the skies and blaspheming man. He screamed to the skies, searching for God, looking to find where he had gone. Burke had a question – really, he just wanted to ask *any* question and hear a response just to know that God still listened. He whimpered, and moaned:

"Where did you go?"

Then, he waited for a response.

Genesis 1:

In the beginning, God created the heavens and the earth. The earth was without form, and void; and darkness was on the face of the deep. And the Spirit of God was hovering over the face of the waters.

Burke cringed at the thought of such a verse. What had happened, what *man* had done, was create a darkness over the face of the deep all by themselves. They had destroyed the firmament beneath their feet and created a dark hole all on their own. And somehow, *God* claimed in the beginning of his book that he was still over the void and the darkness of the waters. Burke wondered if, in that moment when they dropped the bomb, God didn't just turn away for a moment, or if he sat above the darkness and just watched it all unfold from over the waters. Then Burke wondered if God ever really was over the void at all, or if he wasn't just locked up in heaven, oblivious to what man was even doing on earth. How could he even care?

John began to wade out into the dark waters of the Pacific and looked to the east. Somewhere out in the east was the west. *When did I leave the west and end up in the east,* he wondered. *How did I get here?* He trembled. Tears began to roll down his face. Inside, he twisted and turned in all directions until eventually, he could hold it no longer.

"I WANT TO GO HOME!" he shouted as hard as he could.

He fell to his knees in the waters, the waves lapping up hard against his chest. *What if I had gone back,* he wondered. *What if I had left with Major Lowrie and Corporal Harrison? Would things have been different? Would Kioshi — Oh God, Kioshi — would he still be alive, along with the other villagers? Or would I have been in that plane that did Japan in? Would I have been the smoking gun?* The questions rattled on and he found it hard to do anything but cry. His brain ran a hundred miles an hour and his heart beat slowly and sporadically in quiet aches for the lives lost. Hundreds of thousands were vaporized, gone. It was as if they were erased from the earth completely, all recollection of them gone. And all Burke could seem to think about was, "What if?" It was as if he felt that his cowardice in staying behind in Japan had caused the explosion. *What if I wasn't so weak? What if I could have stopped this?*

In that moment, Burke felt the weight of his cowardly decision to stay. Certainly, he saved Kioshi's life, but only for a brief moment. He could not keep Kioshi safe. He could not keep anyone safe, not Leo or Hector or even Lucky. As he wallowed in the ocean,

Burke realized how weak he really was. There was nothing he could save, hardly even himself. And in truth, he realized that he had run away from every major battle he had ever faced. He ran from the enemy over the ocean, he ran from the Japanese once shot down and at the camp, he ran from fighter planes, he ran from home – he was a weak man who just ran.

Suddenly, from behind, something broke through his pain and grabbed him by the arm. It slipped neatly between his arm and his body, as if helping him get up. John rose, turning around to see who was there. There wasn't a soul. Not a person. He touched his arm; sure of what he had felt. It was then, from the darkened skies above, that a ray from the sun broke through the clouds and penetrated the beach with light. It was a faint light, dulled by the grey, ashy earth it touched. But there was light.

Burke hobbled towards the illuminated beach, still weary and haggard. He clung to his arm, as if the feeling of being touched was still there. Not a soul moved about the beach and in the distance, the earth smoldered in heaps of rubble. But the day had not worn down; there was still more yet to go and he had no choice but to go back and help.

August 1945 changed John Burke. He thought of himself as a totally inadequate weakling. But he still owed a debt to someone for the grace they showed him. And that is when it struck him – no matter how long he lived or what he saw, the debt of saving his life could never be repaid, but it didn't matter. He had to keep going, and that is what he did.

SIX

They stood over the dry, cold gravestone, beneath which was an empty and vacant grave for a tiny body that they would never recover. Ayame stood over it, whispering a prayer over a cluster of prayer beads she had wrapped around her knuckles. The gravestone was a small, simple stone, only about a foot and a half tall with writing scrawled crudely by a hammer and dull chisel. There were now *two* names on the gravestone when there used to only be *one*. It was August 13, 1945. The sky was calm; the air was cold.

Ayame, John, and several of the soldiers in the camp who came out of respect for Ayame arrived at the village earlier that morning. There was an eerie calm about the village. Nothing stirred or moved. The only life that remained there was a wild dog that came out only to see what the group of people were doing before scampering off into the woods in search of food. The huts and makeshift homes that scattered the area were vacant of all the villagers' belongings and things. During all the war, Burke had never seen a village vacated with all of the buildings still intact. He had only seen villages pounded by explosions or fire until they were leveled to the ground. In some respects, it was almost worse to see it vacated and standing; it didn't feel right at all.

After the group had arrived at the village, Ayame took them over to her hut so she could get a few things she needed. The two soldiers and Burke stood outside of her hut waiting for her to return. They did not say a thing to each other, keeping their eyes on the ground in front of them. For the first time since John had been there, the guards made no attempt to sneer or hiss at him. The three of them all seemed to have an understanding about the way they felt about things. It did not matter that the nations had made them sworn enemies; with the pain of the blasts only a week before, any aggression or hostility towards one another seemed pointless. When Ayame returned, she motioned for them all to follow her up the sloping hillside behind her hut. She carried in her hands a child-sized kimono, prayer beads, and a chisel and hammer.

They all followed Ayame up the hillside a hundred yards or so. They were close enough to the top of the hill that they could see most of the village beneath them. John and the other men looked down at the village remorsefully, almost regretfully. Ayame glided past them to some trees nearby. "Kuru," she said to them, motioning for them to follow.

The three men followed her behind the trees and into a small clearing where a single headstone sat underneath the light of the sun. There was already scrawling printed on the headstone – "明彦" which stood for "Akihiko," meaning bright prince. Ayame bent down and touched the headstone tenderly, whispering condolences to it quietly.

"Was that her husband," John asked one of the guards quietly. "*Shujin?*" The guard nodded and returned his focus to Ayame and the headstone.

Ayame then carefully picked up the hammer and chisel and lifted them up against the stone. Tears welled up and began to fall down her tired, haggard face. The trembling in her hands had gotten worse and the hammer and chisel shook wildly against the rock. Swooping in, one of the guards bent down beside her and offered to chisel the letters for her. She conceded and whispered to him what to write. After several minutes of carefully, painstakingly carving the letters, the soldier had finished writing. "淳" standing for "Kioshi," meaning pure.

The soldier finished and cleared away the dust from the stone. As Ayame approached, he rose respectfully and let her come before the grave. Ayame bent down and laid out Kioshi's kimono on the ground before the headstone. In a soft voice, she began her prayers, bringing up the prayer beads to her face and bending down over the grave in reverence. The men, including John bent their heads down in respect. Burke felt the streams of tears make trails across his face and watched as they fell gently off his chin and onto his shoe. Eventually, Ayame stood up, wiping the tears from her cheeks, and stepped back from the grave. The four of them stood in complete silence before the foot of the grave.

As the years passed from the time of Kioshi's burial, Burke only felt more and more compassion for Ayame. John was anything but perfect. He certainly wasn't a perfect father either. He had seven children in all: the first three children came from his first marriage, the next three were his second wife's children, and the seventh was between he and his second wife. He did love his children greatly – in fact more than anything. They had all weathered through some fierce storms together and survived. It was never very pretty the way he showed love to his kids but it was love nonetheless. The one thing he knew about every single one of his children, beyond a shadow of a doubt, was that if he ever had to bury one of them, well, he never was quite sure how he would wake up the next morning.

Even as Burke's children became adults, he worried about them just as much as when they were kids. He had one child working on a pipeline in the Gulf of Mexico for years, actually *living* on the water as if a sane person would actually *choose* to do such a thing. His youngest one always worried him. She was so much younger than all the rest and was so gullible. One time, one of the older siblings convinced the youngest that she was adopted from a tribe in Africa. The story would have made John sick knowing she was so gullible if it had not been so funny. Every night, if one of his children was out late past curfew and had not called, or even when a couple of them decided to run away, John stayed up waiting for them until his eyes got weak and his legs buckled from exhaustion. He was never perfect, and he never claimed to be either. But he loved his children unto his death. With seven kids he worried about constantly, he died one tired, old man.

Ayame, though, never had the chance to worry over a child. She would never grow weary by her child's complaining or risk-taking. She would never have to stay up late thinking the worst if he was out past curfew. John thought of this from time to time, later in life. Especially on nights where he would stay up late waiting for one of his children to come home, he would think about Ayame. He knew she was somewhere out there, not getting the chance to stay up late waiting for her child to come home. In fact, she had no home for them to come home *to*. The entire population of her village had vanished in a split second underneath gray and foggy skies. The day they buried Kioshi, Burke cried more for Ayame than he did for losing Kioshi. Little Kioshi no longer had to grow up in a world that wanted to kill him or see him harmed for reasons he couldn't control. Ayame, though, buried a son – who she would have gladly died for – and she never again got to worry over him.

John remembered the day they buried Kioshi every time he looked at the Japanese flag in his dining room. That was what angered him when his daughter brought over her hippie nitwit twit who started reading the flag *out loud*. The kid cocked his head that day and stared at the flag with his little beady eyes like it belonged in a gallery or something. Adjusting his round, smudgy glasses , the kid hunched forward trying to read it.

"Goreizen ni osonae kudasai," the kid read.

"What are you doing?" Burke asked him quickly and nervously, noticing what it was the kid was reading.

"Yeah, I think that is how you pronounce that symbol. Or maybe it's 'kudasi…'"

"That's good enough," Burke told him.

"Daddy," one of his daughters said. "He just wants to read it. It's not going to kill you to let him read it, would it?"

In truth, it would. Burke had never told anyone what had happened in Japan, at least not all of it. It was a chapter left untold and he wanted it that way. It was too dark. Too much. Too hard. And now, a nitwit university kid was about to unravel it all. And there the kid stood, mumbling to himself remarks of great insight while reading the flag.

"Isn't there somewhere you need to go?" John asked the kid curtly.

"Nah," he replied. "We can be late." The kid kept reading.

"I think that's enough!" Burke said, growing more agitated.

"Let's see…" the kid continued. "Oh, I see, the flag is upside-down, no wonder it was so hard." He cocked his head to read it upside-down and brought John's daughter closer, ready to impress her. "Makes more sense now. So this symbol is 'memori-nai' and it is in dedication to…" the kid stopped reading. He took two steps back and looked at the flag as a whole, from a distance. "Holy crap," he whispered to himself. The kid had seen this kind of flag in one of his hoity-toity classes. It was a special kind of the flag, the kind of flag that was hard to get because the only way to get it would be as a gift from someone who loved you. Burial flags like this were not easy to come by, even during the war. And there was no mistake that it was indeed gifted to John – there was him name scrawled at the bottom of the flag.

John glared at the kid in the eyes angrily – the flag had not been read out loud in decades. It wasn't meant to be, not to John it wasn't. He knew what it said – he didn't need to be told and nobody needed to know – and this kid just came in guessing symbols from the flag flippantly like it were a game show or something.

John's daughter looked cluelessly at the two men, waiting for an interpretation. She never got one. Eventually the nitwit kid fumbled around his words before nodding and saying goodbye to Burke, ushering his date out the door. The kid knew where Burke had gotten the flag from and mostly likely *how* he had gotten it. Burke always wanted his family to know the truth, deep down, but he knew that telling them would mean exposing his cowardice – that he stayed behind on purpose. He went AWOL. He didn't want to tell them that, not in the slightest. On the surface, he was afraid that telling them would have hurt their faith in him or in their country. He was afraid that his family would have stopped loving him and would have seen him as a sham. They all held the belief that their father/grandfather/husband/friend was a decorated war hero who was held captive on the island for several years. The truth was, though, that after they had broken out of prison on Mount Sefuri, the only person keeping Burke on that island was himself. It wasn't until he was old, too old to even tell the story, that he realized he was a lot stronger back then than he ever thought he was.

He stayed. And he saved a life.

Back in 1945, at Kioshi's gravesite, Ayame, the guards, and Burke all stood together in silence and in reverence. As they did, one of the soldiers eventually walked forwards, in front of the rest, and turned around to face Ayame. He opened up a sack that he had been carrying with him and from it he took out a Japanese flag. The soldier opened up the flag and showed it to Ayame; on either side of the rising sun were scrawlings in Japanese. They read:

我々は、故人の魂のために祈りを捧げる

虚子のメモリ内

It translated to:

We offer a prayer for the soul of the deceased.

In memory of Kioshi

Ayame came to tears again. Slowly, the soldier folded up the flag and gave it to her. She took it, wiping the tears from her eyes, and thanked the soldier who bowed his head and moved back alongside the other soldier. Ayame kept hold of the flag for a moment. Suddenly, Ayame gracefully bent down and pulled out a pen and ink from some of her belongings. Still shaking in grief, she wrote some additional words on the bottom of the flag:

ありがとジョン

meaning simply *"Thank you John."*

Ayame then rose with the flag in hand and turned to John. Quickly, John moved his gaze away from her, keeping his eyes on the ground below in respect for her.

When she was a few feet away, she stopped, bowed at his feet, extended her arms out to him, and set the flag at his feet. Her bow was so sincere it was as if she was carrying a weight of respect around her neck for Burke. She then looked up at him directly while still on the ground and, with tears coming to her eyes, said, "Thank...you...fo' saving... my... boy. Forever... indebted. Watashi wa anata ni einen ni on."

John looked at the other soldiers, wondering what to do. Despite their shock at Ayame's act, they both nodded as if to tell him to take the flag. Slowly, Burke bent down and picked up the flag that lay at his feet. He then reached out to Ayame who was kneeling below him still and, as best he could, said, "Arigato... Yubi... thank you for your grace, for saving *me.*"

Burke kept the flag until the day he died. It held a reverence in his heart forever. The flag reminded him of all the bitter destruction, death, and pain that he saw during the war; such memories never allowed him to sleep well again. But the flag also reminded him of the coward he once was, and of the weakness it took for him to understand his usefulness. The flag that hung in his dining room for so many years was given to him for saving the life of a boy who, in turn, saved his soul.

Burke, the weak coward, stayed in Japan. And yet, the weak coward saved a life by offering his own which, perhaps, is what truly saved his own soul.

SEVEN

As Burke returned to the base on Nobeoka with the others, he immediately noticed Lieutenant Colonel Mukai standing by the shore, gazing out onto the darkening ocean. Somewhere deep inside, Burke felt compelled to go over and offer him something. He didn't know what it was he had to offer, but he knew he had to do it; he had to do something... anything.

He approached the Lieutenant Colonel slowly, carrying a pack containing the burial flag Ayame had given to him with its corners bulging out of the top of the knapsack. Mukai made no effort to look behind to see who was approaching him; he simply bowed his head and caught John out of the peripherals of his eye. Burke shrunk back a step as Mukai glanced; Mukai remained motionless, fixing his gaze back out over the water.

"Do you know how Japan got name?" he asked Burke.

"Sorry?" John replied.

"Do you know how Japan got name? – Land of Rising Sun? It come from Marco Polo. But before Polo, Japan called *Nihon*...

Nihon… When you write it, symbols look like sun coming up over tree. Chinese call us this, how we got name. Call us this because we are furthest east they could go. Made it look to them like the sun come up out of our trees.

"I did not grow up in mountains, around tallest trees," Mukai continued. "I grew up near ocean, like here. I used to stand on beach, watch sun come up over sea many times. Made me feel I saw sun before Chinese see it, like I was first to see it of all people." Mukai bent his head down and kicked the sand along the shoreline, watching the waves retrieve the sand and level it back into the ground. "But now," he said, turning around to look beyond the trees behind them. "Now the trees in our land have been burned down. Now China see right through us."

Mukai began walking past John, heading back towards the base. John started to say something to him. He wasn't quite sure what exactly *to* say. "Sir… I… I-I am… I don't know what to say…"

"Stop," Mukai replied suddenly. "Silence is true friend that never betrays." John closed his mouth and nodded his head understandingly. "I know you are not kind of American I thought you were. You feel you have part of you in Japan, in *Nihon*. But you will never understand our land. Our people. And they will never understand you. It is time you go."

John shook his head. "Back to America?"

"Yes. Go."

"Sir, I don't have anything there for me. I don't even know America anymore."

Mukai cocked his head. "Did you have something *here* before you crash?" he asked. John shook his head solemnly. "It will not be safe for you here now. Not after blast. Go. Take boat."

Burke couldn't tell whether his heart sank or leapt. He didn't really know what he felt, standing there thinking that he was finally going home. He felt that he needed to thank Lieutenant Colonel Mukai. He began to form the words before Mukai stopped him again.

"Do not speak. Just go. We must leave Nobeoka by tomorrow. You cannot come. Leave tonight." The two said no more to each other; there was nothing left to say. Mukai slowly edged away and then broke out into a march back to the base.

The sea lapped up around John's feet, picking up his knapsack. The bag slowly began to drift out with the tide and onto the water. When Burke realized it was gone, he quickly stumbled his way out into the sea, reaching madly for the strap around his knapsack and eventually pulling it on over his and onto his shoulders. By the time he made his way back to shore, sopping wet, Mukai had disappeared into the camp. John never saw him again.

When he left for war, John took a bag with a change of clothes, a toothbrush, and a Bible. He later got a pistol, issued to him by the United States Military. By the time he landed in Japan, he lost everything he had. So by the time he had to leave, he had no real belongings to pack up and take with him back home; he had not had belongings of his own, really, for two years. He had nothing to go home to either, but he knew Mukai was right. If he had made it that far with what little he had, Burke could make it back to America.

And, as Burke found out, he made it to America without having anything to return to either. He ended up having to *find* the things in life that actually mattered back in America and, to his surprise, they were the same things that mattered as he found them in Japan. His children mattered. His desperate desires to keep them safe mattered. Grace mattered.

As he left the beach and walked towards the base one last time, Burke noticed Ayame from a distance, packing her things and readying herself to move. Despite her haggard, tired, and worn face and her crushed and burdened body, she was a graceful and beautiful woman. It was as if for the first time he noticed how beautiful she really was. He stopped, smiled, and appreciated her for a few moments. She bustled around with abundant grace, moving about as if the wind were carrying her to and fro, gently pushing her around the room. As Burke approached, she looked up from packing her small canvas bag with her closest belongings. Her eyes were still pink from the tears she had wept earlier that day. He gave her a polite wave of his hand at the hip and she smiled back at him, welcoming him into her tent.

"I'm leaving," he told her. He knew she wouldn't understand him, but he felt it was only right to say something to her. She acted as if she understood, though. "I know I don't really have a lot to give you… really anything at all. But I wanted to thank you. For everything."

Ayame cocked her head and looked all over Burke's face for an explanation. He searched everywhere he could for one. He wanted so badly to give her something, anything, to show his appreciation. Finally, he put his hand over his heart and said the only thing he could think of.

"Kioshi… in here."

She smiled and touched her own heart. "Kioshi, in here," she replied.

Ayame began to smile as tears began to sneak out of the sides of her eyes. "Arigato," she whispered behind the tears. Burke nodded quietly. He didn't know what else he could give her and he hoped that she knew what he meant. She and her son had given him his heart and it was all he had left to share with her. It wasn't much, but it was everything he had.

John left the island later that night, when the traffic over the water was quiet. He took the small fishing vessel Lieutenant Colonel Mukai had left for him. One of the guards ushered Burke to the boat and untied the rope that docked it to the shore. Ayame followed them to the shore, clutching her hands close to her heart. When the guard kicked the boat out to float over the water, it took Burke a minute to figure out how to get it started. While he was floating, he took the opportunity to wave at Ayame once more. Eventually, he got the boat started and putzed out over the water. The waves beneath him lit up with the glow of the moon and sky was clear and bright with stars overhead. John turned to the shore to see the guard and Ayame still standing there, watching him disappear from their sight into the horizon of the ocean. That was the last time John ever saw them.

At his feet was the knapsack containing Kioshi's burial flag. It had since dried reasonably well after being soaked in the ocean earlier. John set the boat to coast along towards the east with one hand and bent down to pick up the knapsack with the other hand. He took out one corner of the flag from the opening of the sack and ran his hands along a piece of the bottom of the giant, red circle. That was all Burke ever really needed to feel on the flag in order to remember Japan, to remember *Nihon*.

For years after, Burke rarely ever took the flag out of the knapsack he brought it over in, before his children framed it that is. He took the flag out of the sack completely only once while on the boat in the Pacific. John sat on the deck, drifting and bobbing around on top of the dark, deep, ocean and cried for what seemed like hours. It was hard for Burke to think that a child like Kioshi had to die in someone else's war. His emotions got the best of him that first night out on the ocean. He began pounding the deck with his fist as hard as he could in anger. He was enraged, a feeling that felt strange to him. He thought he should have felt sadder for Kioshi, certainly not enraged. The feeling did not sit on him well. And as he was pounding the surface of the boat, crying all alone for Kioshi and Ayame and all of Japan, his knuckles began to bleed. He noticed the blood only after he had been bleeding for some time. By that point it had been smeared all over his hand. Quickly, he tried to compose himself and stand up. As he did, he stumbled and smeared some of the blood across the red circle on the flag. Three small, hardly noticeable smears of blood wiped across the circle of the Rising Sun. Burke looked at the streaks curiously. The blood fell out of sorrow, not anger, and suddenly he realized that inside, he *was* feeling sad about Kioshi, not enraged.

The flag was all he took with him from Japan. He didn't know what he was going to do with it, but he knew he didn't want people to parade it around. If anyone did, it would have meant that Burke would have to admit to going AWOL and to saving the enemy. That was certainly something he *never* had in mind for a war story. When his kids eventually got hold of the flag, he was upset at first. He conceded to their wishes under the premise that there wasn't much more he could do about it. They would never actually know that he went AWOL; they didn't read Japanese so they would have no idea what the flag was really about. Eventually John realized that even if they knew the truth, he wouldn't care. The flag meant more than just going AWOL and saving the enemy. And after seeing it above his dining room table, and griping and complaining that his kids would do such a thing as hang it in a frame, Burke realized that he was secretly glad they had framed it. It humbled him to see it above his table. It reminded him that he didn't get back to America without a little grace.

John floated around on the Pacific for about thirty six hours before getting picked up by a U.S. vessel. When the men spotted Burke, he had long since run out of gas and was in dire need of a hot meal, water, and a shower. Some of the fine sailors pulled Burke back up the U.S. vessel and wrapped a towel around him. John was relatively frail at the time; he had not realized how much weight he had lost until he saw the size of the other men on the ship. His beard had become a scraggly mess as well; it was a wonder he could breathe out of his face at all. Once on the U.S. ship, Burke clung to his knapsack with the flag, holding it close to his heart, and began to laugh, partly out of joy and partly because it was the only thing he could do at the time. The first sailor who came to Burke's aid grabbed him carefully and spoke calmly into his ear:

"You're going to be alright, man. Take it easy. What is your name and rank?"

Hungry, sunburned, and exhausted, Burke muttered: "Lieutena… John Burke… Burke…"

"Lieutenant? Welcome aboard. Glad you're alive."

As they left the fishing vessel, one of the other sailors began to grab the knapsack out of Burke's grasp. "Hey!" Burke shouted, spinning around to slap him and bring the knapsack closer to his chest.

"Woah, calm down there, buddy!" the sailor said.

"Just let him have it," said another. "We need to get out of here."

The sailor let Burke have the sack, weary of him and eyeballing him cautiously. John didn't care what he thought – he was stuck in *Japan* for two years, he felt he deserved some respect. Furthermore, they were sailors – Burke *never* cared what a Navy guy had to think.

The first place they took John was, of course, to sickbay. Immediately, the sailors pumped Burke full of antibiotics and gave him pain pills, which just caused him to pass the antibiotics through his body and straight into the latrine. The nurses in sickbay were not much help and the medicine the doctors prescribed did about as much good as drinking drain cleaner. Suffice it to say, Burke did eventually regain some strength and put on a few pounds. He began looking better, feeling better, and even the top of his head began to grow in some hair like a normal human scalp.

Burke finally got a hot meal, a shave, and a bath on the vessel, and he was never more happy to do so in all his life. He quickly learned to cherish the little things he had missed for two years. Overall, the men spent about two months bobbing around the Pacific, and not a day went by that John didn't think of Japan. The men finally stationed themselves in the Philippines at a U.S. base, although Burke was not quite sure which base it was at first. After being in the Philippines for a few days, they packed their things and took a load of supplies back to the northern Solomons and eventually back to Hawaii.

While Burke was in Hawaii he received a few medals, accolades, and pats on the back. He told a few stories here and there, mostly in bars, about why his head was all banged up and scarred. The stories usually didn't include Kioshi — Burke never wanted to explain that much to the other men. A lot of them asked about his knapsack, which made a regular appearance with Burke, and about the flag inside. Most of them figured it was something Burke had pulled off of a dead soldier while he was in Japan, as if it were a souvenir or something. Burke never corrected any of them and in fact, with every story that was told, he found himself letting on fewer and fewer details. Worry had already begun to set in. *What if they find out that I went AWOL and then I get arrested for staying over there?* he thought. He asked himself this almost all the time, even when he was an old man, long after the war. So for every question he was asked, he only gave the bare minimum, if that, making him a rather crummy storyteller. Eventually, the other men on Hawaii just stopped asking him for stories because they knew it was going to underwhelm them. This, of course, pleased Burke very much.

John spent quite a bit of time on Hawaii. He never much cared for it – too much ocean. He had never had a good relationship with the ocean and he never wanted one. When the time came to leave, Burke stood in the airport looking at the destinations and thought about where to go. He had no intention of staying in Hawaii. He didn't want to go to the coast again either – still too much water. Illinois, his home state, carried too many bad memories. He couldn't seem to settle himself on anywhere in particular. And while he was debating about where he should live, he overhead a couple soldiers talking about that very thing.

"No, no – New York is no good to fly."

"Sure it is! Lots of service, you can go anywhere you want and need!"

"Yeah, but a terrible landing strip."

"You don't say?"

"You want the best flying around? Go to New Mexico. Best damn weather, great airstrip, perfect flying weather."

"Isn't that the place with all the scientists and dirt and what not?"

"Yeah. Trust me, it's the place to go."

Of course, Burke didn't need to hear anymore – he had made his decision midway through their conversation. "Perfect flying" was all he needed to hear. After purchasing a ticket and hitting the skies, Burke was in Albuquerque, New Mexico, happily away from any traces of tropics or ocean. For him, it was perfect and home to the best airstrip a pilot could ask for.

While there, he fell head over heels with a cute girl, married her, had some kids, divorced the gal, and never heard from her again. It wasn't long until he met a beautiful woman, fell in love again, married her, and had a few more children who gave him a couple heart attacks.

Burke had come back from the war with grace, but it took him a while to "get religious," as he put it. He was never sure if those stories the church told him could really save him from hell and all that. However, John figured that someone or something must have saved him in Japan. If it really was the "mercy of God" that saved him then maybe God would save him from hell as well.

John worked hard, put food on the table, and did the best he could with what he had. He found work as a jack-of-all-trades and master of none. He was never anybody special. He never made the front page, and he was okay with that. John had a family, had a full life, a few laughs, and then died in peace at an good, old age. He never lived a grand, expensive, four-star life, and he never wanted to.

To him, that wasn't the point of life anyway. The point of life, for Burke, was to keep going, no matter what. After surviving Japan, Burke eventually figured if there was a God who really did give out grace and mercy, the least he could do in return was to keep going.

And that was exactly what John did.

EPILOGUE

John was babysitting his young grandson who, at the time, wasn't more than five or six years old. As a 70-something year old man, the task was daunting for John, but he figured if he could survive the war, he could survive babysitting grandchildren. To make his task harder, his wife was out running errands, leaving him and his grandson to endure the house all by themselves. Needless to say, it was a tense fight for survival for the two of them.

As all old men do, John fell asleep in his chair while watching the news. When he woke, he discovered to his horror that his grandson was no longer in the room with him. This worried John because he knew from personal experience that 5-year-old boys tend to do nothing good when they are left alone. Quickly, John got up from his seat and began rummaging all over the house for his grandson, calling his name and so on. Eventually he found the boy rummaging through his things in the bedroom.

"What are you doing?" he asked his grandson authoritatively.

The boy looked up at his grandfather with a menacing little

grin and then quickly returned to rummaging through the drawers, tossing everything out onto the floor.

"Son, stop that! Right now!" John shouted.

Defiantly, his grandson threw everything in his grubby little arms down, looked up at his grandfather, and snuffed, "You're not the boss of *me*!"

John stepped back, caught by the moment of his grandson's defiance. Then he looked deep into the child's face; it was twisted with a look of cockiness, as if the boy believed he was truly invincible. John began to smile, only enough to crease the corner of one cheek.

"Who do you think you are, son?" he asked the boy.

The boy looked back curiously. "I'm... I'm... I'm da boss!" he replied excitedly, showing his big muscles to his granddad in true, macho fashion.

John let go of the smile he had held back, letting himself grin from ear to ear. The boy laughed too and quickly ran to his grandfather's leg, hugging it tightly as John patted the boy's head and surveyed the damage in the room.

"Come along, boss. Let's pick this up."

John sat down on the side of his bed and helped his grandson organize everything back into their respective drawers. As they were taking care of the mess, the boy took hold of an old picture in a battered frame and sat next to his grandfather. John looked over the boy's shoulder at the photo: an old Army photo of Burke from when he enlisted.

"Who's that?" the boy asked.

"That was me, when I was in the Army a looonng time ago," replied John.

"You look skinnier," the boy chirped.

"Yeah, well—"

"And you had hair then."

"Yes, I did."

"What happened to your hair?" the boy asked.

John wondered what he should tell the boy. For years, he only shared the bare minimum. The story usually consisted of an accident and "experimental" surgery in Japan. He never even *dreamed* about telling the rest. But as the boy looked up at his grandfather with his young, bright, blue eyes, John wondered if he shouldn't tell him more. *What if I never had the chance to say it?*

"Well, you know how your mom has told you I was a prisoner in Japan a long, long time ago?" John started.

The boy nodded, wide-eyed.

"Well, I hit my head while I was over there and the Japanese people, well, they saved my life. They put a metal plate in my head to keep me alive."

"How'd it happen?" the boy asked.

John paused. "I was trying to save someone I—I cared for very much."

"Did you save them?"

"Well no," John said. Then he thought for a moment. "I mean, yes. Actually, yes I did. For a time."

"Wooow…" the boy replied. "How long were you there?"

"Oh, a looonng time," John said.

"What was the *grossest* thing that ever happened to you EVER!?"

John smiled at his grandson's brilliant mind. "I ate a lot of raw fish," he told the boy. "Sometimes, they would take the fish right out of the water and kill it and then make us eat it completely raw, eyeballs and all!"

"Ew, gross!" the boy replied, sticking out his tongue in disgust. "What was your favorite part of being over there?" he continued.

John had to really think about the boy's question. He had never been asked to name a "favorite part" of being a prisoner in a foreign country, and he wasn't really sure how to answer that without going into detail. Eventually, John replied with the first thing that came to mind. "The geishas," he said with a laugh.

"What's a gay-sha?" the boy asked.

His grandfather let out a great chuckle. "It's nothing, don't worry about it, son. And don't ask your mother either! You don't want to get me in trouble."

"Okay, Poppy," the boy said, jumping off the bed and putting up the photo. "Poppy? Did you ever have to kill anyone?" he asked.

John stopped, his face turning somber and discouraged. "Did I ever kill anyone?"

"It's okay if you did. We talked about war in class and Mrs. Coll said that sometimes things like dying happens in war. Logan's grandpa was in a war and talked to him about killing people. That's why Mrs. Coll talked to us."

"Oh, well, uhm, that sort of thing does happen sometimes."

The boy wiped his running nose with the edge of his sleeve, smearing snot all over his shirt. "Mom told me that you saved us back then, that you saved a lot of people. Did you?"

"I- uhm, I guess I did," John said. He had not really thought about it much since the war. *I wished I could have saved more,* he thought.

"Did you ever save any Japanese people?" the boy prodded again.

Standing up, weak at his knees, John thought about telling the boy the same lie he had been telling for years. However, there stood his grandson, a young boy full of innocence and forgiveness. *What does it matter?* he thought. *What if the chance never comes again?*

"Yes," John said. "I did save some Japanese people."

The boy bobbed back and forth on his feet, looking up at his old grandpa, eyes full of respect and love. "That's cool..." the boy began. "Thanks, Poppy." He then scurried back to his grandpa and hugged his leg.

"Thank you for what?" John asked.

"For saving people," the boy replied.

And then John shed a lone tear. For the first time, it was out of pride.

"Can I go play outside!?" the boy quickly shouted, breaking away from his grandfather's leg.

"Sure, kiddo," John told him.

The boy darted out of the room in an excited frenzy, leaving John by himself. He reached over and picked up his old Army picture. He didn't look half bad, he thought to himself. And he didn't do half bad either. He made it through: enlisted, shipped off, shot down, held captive, and runaway. He didn't do half bad.

John lived to be 83 years old. He died, having lived a full, rich life. The flag he used to eat breakfast, lunch, and dinner under was passed on to his son and would later be passed on to his son and so forth. In the end, it no longer reminded John of the things he regretted; of the things he wanted to keep secret. So what if he was a coward who found himself running from everything? He saved a life. He saved it, and he cared for it, and he *loved* it deeply.

Perhaps the bravest thing John ever did in his life was to stay, though he always saw it as cowardice. In truth, he made a decision to keep going. Up to his final days, Burke never stopped asking, "What if I had only tried a little harder, done something different to save him...?" In his final moments on earth, though, he realized it didn't matter. In the end, he fought for life itself, and he didn't give up.

John Oscar Burke always thought himself something of a coward. Perhaps he did what many would consider a cowardly thing, but he did it bravely and faithfully, and that was what made him a hero.

Kyle Ryan Bullock was first published at the age of 8. Since then, he has been writing stories, poetry, and plays about life, love, and family. His other works include *Those Unforgettable Black Rims* and *A History of Wisdom: a parable in one act.* Kyle also administers a blog that shares stories and thoughts about life, love, and family from a variety of writers. Kyle has a degree in psychology and is working on his Master's of Leadership at Lubbock Christian University. He lives with his wife, Devon, in West Texas.

Made in the USA
San Bernardino, CA
14 January 2014